# TOUGH MAN

Lonigan's eyes went to the rifles, then to the riflemen. "You're tryin' to get yourself killed, Hoey. Now take your boys and light a shuck."

Ives chuckled. "Oh, no! We've got our herd. When your boys hear us call, they'll come in. They'll never know what hit' em."

"You mean," Danny Lonigan's voice was casual, "like this?" His hands flashed for his guns, and for one startled instant, every man froze. Then as one person, Ives, Calkins, and Lee grabbed iron.

It was Lonigan's sudden move that decided it. His first two shots knocked Casselman staggering and his third dropped Shain dead in his tracks. "Drop it, Short!" Lonigan yelled, and switched both guns to Papago Brown.

Then, suddenly, it was all over and where the cannonade of guns had sounded there was stillness.

# Bantam Books by Louis L'Amour
## Ask your bookseller for the books you have missed.

### NOVELS

BENDIGO SHAFTER
BORDEN CHANTRY
BRIONNE
THE BROKEN GUN
THE BURNING HILLS
THE CALIFORNIOS
CALLAGHEN
CATLOW
CHANCY
THE CHEROKEE TRAIL
COMSTOCK LODE
CONAGHER
CROSSFIRE TRAIL
DARK CANYON
DOWN THE LONG HILLS
THE EMPTY LAND
FAIR BLOWS THE WIND
FALLON
THE FERGUSON RIFLE
THE FIRST FAST DRAW
FLINT
GUNS OF THE
    TIMBERLANDS
HANGING WOMAN
    CREEK
THE HAUNTED MESA
HELLER WITH A GUN
THE HIGH GRADERS
HIGH LONESOME
HONDO
HOW THE WEST WAS
    WON
THE IRON MARSHAL
THE KEY-LOCK MAN
KID RODELO
KILKENNY
KILLOE
KILRONE
KIOWA TRAIL
LAST OF THE BREED
LAST STAND AT PAPAGO
    WELLS
THE LONESOME GODS
THE MAN CALLED NOON
THE MAN FROM
    SKIBBEREEN
THE MAN FROM THE
    BROKEN HILLS
MATAGORDA
MILO TALON
THE MOUNTAIN VALLEY
    WAR
NORTH TO THE RAILS

OVER ON THE DRY SIDE
PASSIN' THROUGH
THE PROVING TRAIL
THE QUICK AND THE
    DEAD
RADIGAN
REILLY'S LUCK
THE RIDER OF LOST
    CREEK
RIVERS WEST
THE SHADOW RIDERS
SHALAKO
SHOWDOWN AT YELLOW
    BUTTE
SILVER CANYON
SON OF A WANTED MAN
TAGGART
THE TALL STRANGER
TO TAME A LAND
TUCKER
UNDER THE SWEETWATER
    RIM
UTAH BLAINE
THE WALKING DRUM
WESTWARD THE TIDE
WHERE THE LONG GRASS
    BLOWS

### SHORT STORY
### COLLECTIONS

BEYOND THE GREAT
    SNOW MOUNTAINS
BOWDRIE
BOWDRIE'S LAW
BUCKSKIN RUN
DUTCHMAN'S FLAT
END OF THE DRIVE
THE HILLS OF HOMICIDE
LAW OF THE DESERT
    BORN
LONG RIDE HOME
LONIGAN
MONUMENT ROCK
NIGHT OVER THE
    SOLOMONS
THE OUTLAWS OF
    MESQUITE
THE RIDER OF THE RUBY
    HILLS
RIDING FOR THE BRAND
THE STRONG SHALL LIVE
THE TRAIL TO CRAZY MAN
VALLEY OF THE SUN
WAR PARTY

WEST FROM SINGAPORE
WEST OF DODGE
YONDERING

### SACKETT TITLES

SACKETT'S LAND
TO THE FAR BLUE
    MOUNTAINS
THE WARRIOR'S PATH
JUBAL SACKETT
RIDE THE RIVER
THE DAYBREAKERS
SACKETT
LANDO
MOJAVE CROSSING
MUSTANG MAN
THE LONELY MEN
GALLOWAY
TREASURE MOUNTAIN
LONELY ON THE
    MOUNTAIN
RIDE THE DARK TRAIL
THE SACKETT BRAND
THE SKY-LINERS

### THE HOPALONG CASSIDY
### NOVELS

THE RIDERS OF HIGH
    ROCK
THE RUSTLERS OF WEST
    FORK
THE TRAIL TO SEVEN
    PINES
TROUBLE SHOOTER

### NONFICTION

EDUCATION OF A
    WANDERING MAN
FRONTIER
THE SACKETT
    COMPANION:
    A Personal Guide to
    the Sackett Novels
A TRAIL OF MEMORIES:
    The Quotations of Louis
    L'Amour, compiled by
    Angelique L'Amour

### POETRY

SMOKE FROM THIS ALTAR

# LONIGAN
## Louis L'Amour

**BANTAM BOOKS**
NEW YORK · TORONTO · LONDON · SYDNEY · AUCKLAND

## *To Bob Christy*

LONIGAN

*A Bantam Book / published by arrangement with the author*

PUBLISHING HISTORY

*Bantam edition / October 1988*
*Bantam reissue July 1997*
*Author photo by John Hamilton/Globe photos*

ISBN 0-553-27536-4

*Published simultaneously in the United States and Canada*

*Bantam Books are published by Bantam Books, a division of Bantam Doubleday*
*Dell Publishing Group, Inc. Its trademark, consisting of the words "Bantam*
*Books" and the portrayal of a rooster, is Registered in U.S. Patent and Trade-*
*mark Office and in other countries. Marca Registrada. Bantam Books, 1540*
*Broadway, New York, New York 10036.*

PRINTED IN THE UNITED STATES OF AMERICA

OPM    24 . 23   22   21

# Contents

# Foreword

Several of the stories that follow have to do with the large-scale movement of cattle from place to place. In the days of the cattle drives for which the west became famous, those movements usually began in Texas and went north to the railroad shipping towns in Kansas, though cattle were often driven on to northern ranges in Wyoming, Montana, the Dakotas, or Canada.

The largest herd that could be handled with ease—if that term could be applied to any cattle drive—was about 2500 head. A few larger herds were moved, but they proved difficult and so were rarely attempted.

It was customary to move such herds at twelve to fifteen miles per day, and often less, depending on the existing grass and water. The idea was to take time and let the herd fatten up as it moved.

In the days of the early drive the horns on a longhorn would average over four feet wide, and those with horns of six feet and better could be found in almost every herd. There were a few, of course, that exceeded that breadth, but they were the exception.

Stampedes were the bane of the drover's existence for more weight could be run off in a night than could be put on in a week, and aside from the loss of many head of cattle, the weight loss was enough to cut all the profit from such a drive.

The longhorns driven north from Texas were wild animals, rounded up from the plains of eastern Texas and driven from the thickets. Once trail-broken and away from their old grazing grounds, they moved along easily, but at night or when bad weather was breeding, they were easily startled, and once they had stampeded, were easy to start again. Twelve to eighteen men could handle a herd of the size I mention, although the numbers varied. Within a few days, and in some cases a few hours, the herd would sort itself out. One steer, or sometimes a cow, would take the lead and maintain it. The others would string out, and usually the same bunch could be found leading the herd and another lot bringing up the rear.

Unless the next day's drive to water was a long one, a responsible drover would take his time getting the herd off the bedding ground where they had slept the night before, and unless grazing along the route, they were usually stopped for a noon break and permitted to graze and rest.

Usually when on a drive, the cattle would be strung out over several miles of trail, each steer holding to his own place in line. Even after a stampede, as soon as the herd was strung out again, each steer would find his place in line, usually beside some particular companion. Among cattle there were always those who assumed leadership, moving right to the front of the herd and remaining there. Such a one was Old Blue, famous on Texas ranges for many years, who led herd after herd over the trail to Kansas.

If possible, a trail-drive boss would water his herd then move along two or three miles before bedding them down for the night. Such cattle settled down in much better shape and started off better in the morning.

Cattle drives were not all from Texas into Kansas

and farther north. In earlier days herds had swum the Mississippi, and during the war, were driven to southern markets. Other herds had been driven to Chicago and even into Ohio and Pennsylvania. These, however, were infrequent, and most of the drives were from Texas north. It has been estimated that in the space of some fifteen years, more than ten million cattle were driven from Texas.

Cattle were also driven from Oregon into Montana and Wyoming. These were rarely longhorns, but mostly Durham with some Herefords, and relatively less trouble than the longhorn.

There are still cattle drives nowadays, although for shorter distances and with fewer head. And there are always a few volunteer riders to accompany any such drive, men from other occupations who love the experience of the drive, its hard work and friendly associations. My friend Charlie Daniels, leader of the Charlie Daniels Band, is one such.

# AUTHOR'S NOTE
# THE FINE ART OF RUSTLING

*No doubt the rustling of cattle started on the second day after the first cattle ranch was established, and the ingenuity of the rustler has increased over the years. Many of the early wars in Scotland and Ireland were wars over stolen cattle, and many of the customs of western men can be traced to Scottish Highlanders.*

*There was no set pattern of stealing cattle. Of course, the usual way was simply to round up a few cows on the range and drive them off. Another common practice was to simply drift cattle into a remote corner of the range, then, when the occasion offered, nudge them a little farther away, often into some remote canyon where the grass and water were good and the cattle not likely to return to old pastures. In due time the brands would be altered by a good rewrite man and the cattle drifted into the thief's own herd.*

*"Sleepering" cattle was another device. During the round-up, when each ranch was represented by its own hands or perhaps simply a rep—a cowhand representing brands whose hands were not officially involved in the roundup—all cattle were being checked off and the unbranded marked with the appropriate brands and returned to the herd to be released on the range. Rounded up and unbranded cattle were held in a special herd to be branded in following days, and during the night those cow thieves engaged in sleepering would drive some of the unbranded stock over to the branded herd. Later, after the cattle were released on the range, they would cut out and brand the unbranded stock for themselves.*

*At first, when the cattle business was new, beef*

1

had no value and much wild, unbranded, or "maverick" stock ran loose on the range. When the railroad was built into Kansas and there was a demand for beef in the eastern states, cowhands would ride out with a running iron to brand anything they found, and an artist with a simple running iron could create any brand he wished. As the cattle business became big business, running irons were outlawed and only stamp irons were permitted. The stamp iron has a cattleman's brand which can be burned on the side of a steer with one move. Anyone caught with a running iron could be and often was hung simply on suspicion that he was a rustler.

Rustlers, of course, were not to be pushed aside so easily, and many found they could be just as inventive and artistic with a saddle cinch ring, held by two sticks after being heated in a fire, as with a running iron. Some twisted and heated barbed wire did almost as well.

Of course, by killing and skinning the steer, the alteration of a brand could be seen plainly on the inside of the hide. Stock killed for sale to meat markets left a hide to be disposed of where it was not likely to be found. Often such hides were buried, and occasionally found by a rancher with a rope suitable for providing the rustler with a suspended sentence—suspended from the nearest tree.

Down along the border it was for a time the custom to steal cattle in Mexico, and trail them over to sell in the States. Returning, the outlaws would steal cattle in the States to be sold back in Mexico. It is reported that King Fisher of Uvalde, the gunfighter, had a nice operation like this until he reformed and became a deputy sheriff.

Unfortunately he took a trip to San Antonio, and in trying to keep Ben Thompson out of trouble, was killed beside him, leaving a weeping widow and some fatherless cows.

The stories of rustling are many, and new devices are being invented all the while. Although horse-riding bandits are out of fashion now, the stealing of cattle is not, only now it is done with trucks.

# Lonigan

Heat lay like the devil's curse upon the slow-moving herd, and dust clouded above and around them. The eyes of the cattle were glazed, and the grass beneath their feet was brown and without vigor or life-giving nourishment.

The sun was lost in a brassy sky, and when Calkins knelt and put his palm to the ground the earth was almost too hot to touch. He got slowly to his feet, his face unnaturally old with the gray film of dust and the stubble of beard on his jaws.

"You ask for the truth." His voice was harsher than normal, and Ruth Gurney recognized it at once, and looked at him quickly, for as a child, she had known this man and had loved him like an uncle. "All right, you'll get the truth. There's no chance of you making money on this herd. Half your cows will die this side of Dodge. They'll die of thirst and heat, and the rest won't be worth the drive. You're broke, ma'am."

Her lips tightened and as the truth penetrated she was filled with desperation coupled with a feminine desire for tears. All along she had guessed as much, but one-and-all the hands had avoided telling her.

"But what's the matter, Lon? The Circle G always made its drives before, and always made money. We've the same men, and the trail's the same."

"No." He spoke flatly. "Nothin's the same. The trail's bad. It's been a strikin' dry year, and we got a late start. The other herds got the good grass, and trampled the rest into the dust. She's hotter'n usual, too. And," he added grimly, "we ain't got the same men."

"But we have, Lon!" Ruth protested.

"No." He was old and stubborn. "We ain't. We got one new one too many, and the one we should have ain't here."

Her lips tightened and her chin lifted. "You mean Hoey Ives. You don't like him."

"You should spit in the river, I don't! Nor do the others. He's plumb bad, ma'am, whether you believe it or not. He's no-account. I'll allow, he's educated and slick talkin', but he's still an Ives, and a bigger pack of coyotes never drew breath."

"And you think this—this Lonigan would make a difference? What can one man do against heat and dust and distance? What could he do to prevent storms and rustler raids?"

"I ain't for knowing. If'n I did, mebbe this herd would get through in shape. But Lonigan would know, and Lonigan would take her through. Nor would he take any guff from Hoey Ives. I'll tell you, ma'am, Hoey ain't along for fun. He comes of a pack of outlaws, and education ain't changed his breed none."

"We won't talk about Mr. Ives any further, Lon. Not one word. I have utmost confidence in him. When the drive is over I . . . I may marry him."

Lon Calkins stared at her. "I'll kill him first, or die shooting. Your pappy was a friend of mine. I'll not see a daughter of his marry into that outfit." Then he added, more calmly. "If'n that's what you figure, Ruth, you better plan on hirin' new hands when you get back to Texas."

"Very well, then, that's what I'll do, Lon." Her voice was even, but inside her words frightened her. "That's just what I'll do. I own the Circle G, and I'll run it my way."

Calkins said nothing for a long minute, and then he mused. "I wonder sometimes if'n anybody does *own* a brand. The Circle G, ma'am, ain't just a brand on some cows. It ain't just some range in Texas. It's more . . . much, much more.

"I ain't much hand to talkin' of things like that, but you remember when your pappy and us come west? The Comanches killed O'Brien and Kid Leslie on the Brazos. I reckon both of them were part of the Circle G, ma'am. And Tony, that lousy Italian grub hustler, the one who rolled under a chuck wagon down on the cowhouse. He was part of the Circle G, too.

"A brand ain't just a sign on a critter, it's the lives, and guts, and blood of all the men that went to build it, ma'am. You can't get away from that, no way. The Circle G is your pappy standin' over your mother when she died givin' birth to you. The Circle G is all of that.

"Nobody owns a brand, ma'am, like I say; nobody. It's a thing that hangs in the air over a ranch, over its cows, and over its men. You know why that kid Wilkeson got killed in Uvalde? An hombre there said this was a lousy outfit, and the kid reached for his gun. He died for the brand, ma'am, like a hundred good and bad men done afore this. And you want to wipe it out, destroy it, just because you got your mind set on a no-account coyote. I wish Lonigan was back."

"Lonigan!" She burst out furiously. "All you talk about is Lonigan! *Who* is he? *What* is he? What difference can one man make?"

"Well," Calkins said grimly, "your pappy made a sight of difference! If'n he was with this drive now, your fancy Hoey Ives would pack out of here so fast his dust would be bigger'n that raised by the herd! Or if Lonigan was. Fact is," he added grimly, "there ain't nary a cowhand down there wouldn't draw on Hoey tomorrow if'n he figured he had a chance. Hoey's killed ten men, all better'n him except with a gun."

"And yet you think Lonigan could beat him?" she asked wryly.

"Mebbe. I ain't sure, but I am sure of one thing. If Lonigan died you can bet your boots Hoey Ives would die with him! You say," he continued, "what difference can one man make? Well, he can make a sight of difference. Lonigan doesn't talk so much; he's a good worker, but he's got something in him, something more'n most men. He ain't so big, rightly he's not, but he *seems* big, and he rode for the brand, Lonigan did. He loved the Circle G. Loved it like it was his own."

"Then where is he now when we need him?" Ruth demanded bitterly. "This . . . this superman of yours. Where is he now? You say he never missed a trail drive, that he would drift off, but somehow like he knew the day and hour, he would show up and take his place with the herd. Where is he now?"

"Mebbe he's dead." Calkins was grim. "Wherever he is, he's with the Circle G, and we're with him."

They looked up at the sound of hoofs, and Lon Calkins's face tightened grimly. Abruptly, he reined his horse around. "I'll be ridin'," he said.

"You meant what you said about quitting?" she asked.

"If he stays," Calkins insisted, "I go."

"I'll be sorry to lose you, Lon. The Circle G won't be the same without you."

His old eyes met hers and he stared at her. "Believe me, it won't. Your father should have had a son."

He rode away then, and she stared after him, her body feeling empty as an old sack. The approaching hoofs drew nearer and slowed, and her eyes turned with relief toward those of Hoey Ives.

\*　　\*　　\*

He was a big young man with hard black eyes in which she had never seen the cruelty or calculation that lay in their depths He rode magnificently and was a top hand. On this trip he had been her mainstay, ramrodding it through, talking to lift her spirits, advising her and helping her in countless ways. It was he who had selected the trail they took, he who had ridden out alone to meet the rustlers that would have stopped them, and who talked them out of trouble.

"What's the matter with the old man?" he asked. "What's he growling about now?"

"Oh, he was talking about the old days on the Circle G," she said, "and about Lonigan."

"Lonigan?" Hoey's gaze sharpened, and for an instant she seemed to read apprehension in his eyes. "He hasn't heard from him?"

"Nobody has. Yet he always made the drive."

"He's dead," Ives replied. "He must be. I knew he always made the drive, and that was why I waited before offering my services. We never got along, you see."

"What's he like?" she asked curiously.

"Lonigan?" Ives hesitated, while his bay stamped its foot restlessly. "He's a killer. Utterly vicious."

"But the boys liked him," Ruth protested.

"Sure. He was their pride and joy," Ives said bitterly. "He led the Circle G parade. No man, not even your father, had as much influence with the hands. He was loudmouthed and a braggart, but he appealed to them, and they found excuses for his killings."

"Yet he must have something . . . ?"

"Yes," Hoey Ives nodded reluctantly. "He had that. There was something about him, something that frightened men who didn't even know him." . . .

Ives rejoined the herd, and Ruth Gurney rode on, lingering along the hillcrests away from the dust, watching the herd that meant everything to her. The sale of that herd could mean the ranch was out of debt, that it was hers, all hers. Yet she knew that what Calkins had said was true, bitterly true. Not half the herd would live to see Dodge, and she would be broke then, broke and finished.

She turned her horse and put him on up the slope to the very top of the long, low hill that ran beside the trail. On top there might be more breeze. And there was, although but little more. Yet she sat her horse there, looking over the brown, trampled-down grass that stretched on beyond it. There, too, the herds had been. The earlier herds that had started sooner.

The failure of Lonigan to appear had caused most of that delay. All along she had realized why Calkins was waiting, why the hands kept looking toward the trail, why they found excuses to ride into town, why they intercepted every drifting horseman to ask about him, but for the first time he had not appeared.

She pushed on across the ridge, riding due west. The sun was already far down toward the horizon but it was still unbearably hot. Heat waves danced and rippled against the sky along the ridges, and she slowed her horse to a walk and pushed on alone, lost now from the herd, with only the rising dust to mark its presence.

Half asleep, lulled by the heat and the even rhythm of the walking horse, she dozed in the saddle, and then the horse stopped and coolness touched her face. She was atop another ridge, and far toward the west she seemed to see a thin edge of green, and then her eyes dropped and she saw the tracks of a horse. The horse was shod and the tracks were fresh.

Without doubt the tracks were no more than an hour old, two hours at most. In that time the herd had moved less than three miles, so its dust cloud would have been within sight. Why had the strange rider avoided them?

His horse had stopped here on this ridge, and from the tracks he must have watched the dust cloud. It was unusual for a rider to be so close and not to approach the herd. Unless—she frowned and bit her lip—unless he was an outlaw.

She realized instantly that she should ride to the herd and let Calkins know. Rather, let Hoey Ives know. It might be another raid, and rustlers had already hit them for over three hundred head of stock. Nevertheless, her curiosity aroused, she turned her horse and started backtracking the man.

From time to time she paused to rise in her stirrups and look carefully around the prairie, yet nowhere could she see anything, not a sign of a rider beyond the tracks she followed. Aware that it was time to turn back, she pushed on, aware that the terrain was changing and that she was riding into a broken country of exposed ledges and sharp upthrusts of rock. Topping a rise, she drew up, frowning.

Before her lay a long green valley, several miles wide and grassy and well watered. This was the green, some of the grass showing from the hilltops, that she had seen from some distance east. What a waste to think their herd was passing over that miserable brown and dusty plain when all this was going to waste! It was too bad Hoey did not know of this.

She pushed on to the bottom of the valley and toward a water hole, the tracks for the moment forgotten. And then at the water hole she saw them again. Here the rider had stopped, a tall man with rundown bootheels and Mexican spurs, judging by the tracks in the sand.

She was lying on her stomach drinking when her eyes lifted in response to the sudden falling of a shadow. She saw shabby boots and the Mexican spurs, dark leather chaps, and then a slim-waisted man wearing a faded red shirt and a black kerchief around his throat. His hat was gray, dusty, and battered.

"Hello," he said, smiling at her. "You've got water on your chin."

She sprang to her feet irritably and dashed a quick hand across her mouth and chin. "Suppose I have? What business is it of yours?"

His face was browned from sun and wind, his eyes faintly whimsical. He wore, she noticed suddenly, two guns. He was rolling a cigarette, and now he placed it carefully in the corner of his mouth and struck a match left handed. For some idiotic reason she suddenly wished the wind would blow it out. It didn't.

His eyes slanted from her to her horse and the brand. "Circle G," he murmured thoughtfully, "I reckon that's a Texas outfit."

"If you were from Texas," she replied with asperity, "you would know. There wasn't a better known cattleman in Texas than Tom Gurney!"

"Relative of his?"

"His daughter. And my herd is just a few miles east of here."

"Yeah," his voice was suddenly sarcastic, "that's what comes of a woman ramroddin' a herd. You got your stock on dry grass with this valley offerin' shelter, graze, and plenty of water."

"For your information," she said coldly, "I'm not ramrodding the herd. My trail boss is. He evidently did not know of this valley."

"And evidently he didn't try very hard to find out about it. You got a lousy trail boss, ma'am."

"I didn't ask you! Mr. Ives is—" She was startled by the way his head came up.

"Did you say . . . *Ives*? You don't mean Hoey Ives?"

"I do. You . . . you know him?"

"I should smile. Your dad must be dead, then . . . for he'd never let an Ives ramrod a trail herd of his, else."

"Who are you?" she demanded. "You talk like you knew my father?"

He shrugged. "You know this country. Folks pass

stories along from camp to camp. A man can know a lot about a country without ever bein' there. I'm just from Wyoming."

Suddenly, he glanced up. "Cloudin' up for sure. You'll never make it back to the herd now before the rain comes. Mount up and we'll go down to the cabin."

She looked at him coldly, then cast an apprehensive glance at the sky. "I'll race the storm to the herd," she said coolly. "Thanks just the same."

"No," he said, "you'd never make it. I know these prairie thunderstorms. There may be hail, and sometimes the stones are big enough to beat your brains out. The cabin is closer."

Even as he spoke, there was a rumble of thunder and a few spattering drops landed near them. Worriedly, she glanced at the sky. It was dark and lowering. She had been so preoccupied by the tracks and then by the valley that she had not noticed the rising clouds. Now she saw that there was indeed a bad storm coming, and recalling some of the gullies she had traversed she knew that the trail back would be fraught with danger. She glanced once at the strange rider, hesitated, then said swiftly, "All right, we'll go."

"We'd better make a run for it!" he said, swinging into the saddle. "She'll drop the bottom out of the bucket in a minute!"

Following his lead, she dashed off downstream at breakneck, reckless speed. Yet when they swept around the corner near the cabin his hand went up, and he turned toward her, his face dark and hard. With a gesture, he indicated several horses in the corral, and smoke rising from the ancient chimney. "This could be trouble!" he said grimly. "There was nobody here an hour ago, and nobody rides loose in this country right now who's honest!"

"Including yourself?" she asked quickly.

His grin was lopsided but not without humor.

"Maybe even me," he agreed, "but you back me in whatever I say. Good or bad men, we need shelter!"

Swiftly they unsaddled their horses and led them to the stable. There was still room for two or three horses, indicating that some of the riders were less than particular about their mounts. Then the strange rider led the way toward the cabin. Out of the corner of his mouth, he said, "Call me Danny!"

He pushed the door open and stepped inside, the girl right behind him. He had known they would be observed and that the men within the cabin would have worked out some sort of plan if they were not honest men, and his first glance told him they were not. "How's for some grub?" he asked coolly. "We got caught in the rain!"

A big man standing with his back to the fireplace grinned. "Got caught in good company, I see! Ain't often a feller gets hisself caught out with a girl in these parts!"

"Especially," Danny said quietly, "when she's his boss!"

"Boss?" The big man's eyes sharpened. "Never heard tell of no woman cow boss!"

"You heard of one now." There were four men in the room, and two of them Danny recognized at once. Neither Olin Short nor Elmo Shain were names unknown to the law of half a dozen states and territories. The big man he did not know, nor the lean saturnine man with the scarred face. "This is Ruth Gurney, boss of the Circle G."

The big man stiffened and peered hard at her, then at Danny. "You don't look familiar to me," he said. "I figured I knowed the G riders."

"Then if you don't know me," Danny said quietly, "you ain't known 'em long."

Olin Short, who was neither short nor fat, glanced up. "Here's coffee for the lady," he said quietly. "You pick up a cup and rinse her under the rainspout . . . if'n you're particular."

Danny took the cup and without hesitation stepped
to the door and rinsed the cup. When he stepped back
inside his eyes sought Olin's face. The man was about
thirty, not a bad-looking man with blue eyes and a
stubble of beard. If there was one among them upon
whom he might place some trust, it was Short.

"How far off's the G?" It was the scarred man who
spoke.

Danny glanced at him. "Maybe six miles," he lied,
"not over ten."

"Know where you are?"

Danny nodded. "Why not? Miss Gurney was riding an' when the storm started they sent me after her.
I told 'em if we couldn't make it back we'd hole up
here."

"How'd you know about this shack?" Now it was
the big man who spoke, and his voice was suddenly
hard.

Danny filled his cup before replying. "I stopped
here a week once, last winter," he said, "helped some
boys drive some horses into New Mexico."

"Horses? Into New Mexico?" Shain laughed. "I
thought Billy the Kid and his outfit had that sewed up."

"It was Billy's outfit." Danny spoke quietly and
without seeming to notice the sudden shock on their
faces. When they spoke again, however, there was new
respect on their faces.

"Billy's outfit, huh? Who was with him?"

"Jesse Evans, Hendry Brown, and a couple of other
hombres. They had the horses, and I was drifting toward
Cimarron, but joined up with them and drove down to
the Ruidoso instead."

The reply seemed to satisfy the men, for no more
questions were asked. Ruth sipped her coffee slowly,
soaking up the warmth of the room. She was sufficiently
aware of the situation in west Texas to know these were
hard, dangerous men. They were outlaws. And this

man with her might be another of the same breed. She had heard of Billy the Kid, the soft-voiced boy of not yet eighteen who already had won a name for deadly gun skill, and of his friend, the man who in time would be on the opposite side, Jesse Evans.

Danny had taken his cup and moved back near the wall. He placed it on the floor and rolled a smoke deftly.

"What happens," the scar-faced man said suddenly, "if you don't show up with the lady come daylight?"

"Why, I reckon there'd be eight or ten of the toughest hands in Texas riding thisaway to find out why," Danny said quietly. Then his eyes lifted, and they seemed to blaze with sudden fire. The quiet was gone from them, and from his voice, which carried an edge that was sharp and clean. "But don't worry . . . we'll ride into that camp come mornin'. Nobody," he said, more quietly, "or nothing, will keep us from it."

Shain stared at him, sitting up from the wooden bunk where he had been reclining. "You talk plumb salty, stranger. Who are you? Maybe you are the Kid?" he sneered.

Danny smiled, suddenly. "Why, you boys been around here before, I take it," he said coolly. "If you were, maybe you'll recall the calling cards I left here. You see, I came back this way after that trip to Lincoln and the Ruidoso . . . and had occasion to leave some reminders."

Elmo Shain's sneer was wiped from his face as if by magic, and he shot a quick, horrified glance toward the big man by the fireplace. For some reason that comment electrified the group in the room. Ruth had the feeling that Short alone was pleased.

Conversation died again in the room, and Danny finished his coffee, then refilled both their cups. "Shain," he said suddenly, "when the lady finishes her coffee, how's for lettin' her have that bunk? She's some tired."

At the use of his name, Shain had glanced up

sharply. For a slow minute he said nothing, and then he nodded. "Yeah," he said, "all right."

Danny finished his smoke and rubbed it out. His message had ruined whatever plans they had made, or had at least made them doubt their use. Now they knew either who he was or that he was somebody to be reckoned with. He would have small cause for worry until two of them excused themselves and went outside to talk things over. When they returned he would have to be even more watchful.

Although reluctant to lie down, Ruth suddenly found herself so exhausted that she began to doze almost as soon as she touched the bunk. Danny drew a blanket over her and squatted at the foot of the bunk, his back against the wall.

A slow hour paraded past. The scarred man got up and muttering something about wood for the fire, went out. Shain was asleep, sitting against the wall. The big man followed the scarred man after the wood, and Olin Short threw the last stick on the fire and leaning close to Danny, said quietly, "Watch yourself. The big hombre is Casselman. The mean one is the devil of the lot . . . he's Papago Brown."

"Where do you stand?"

Short's face hardened. "Only to help that girl. I'll see no woman wronged. Least of all, any girl of Gurney's."

"Good."

The door opened and the two men came in and dropped two armfuls of wood near the fireplace. Casselman looked down at her. "Looks mighty purty, lyin' there."

Danny got slowly to his feet. A new cigarette was in the corner of his mouth. "Stay away from her," he said.

Casselman's big head turned to look over his shoulder. He chuckled, a slow, sneering chuckle. "You'd stop me?"

Papago was still near the door. Danny nodded coolly, "I sure would, Casselman. You make a move toward her, and I'll kill you. I'll shoot low down, Casselman, and I couldn't miss.

"As for Papago," he added coolly, "if he doesn't get his hand off that gun butt, I'll kill him now."

Casselman laughed and Brown stared at Danny, smiling. "That stuff about those three skeletons didn't faze us," Papago said. "We're goin' to call your bluff."

"All right," Danny said, "but did you ever hear of Lonigan missing?"

"*Lonigan?*"

At the name, Ruth Gurney was suddenly wide awake. Who had said it? To whom? Papago Brown's face was white and Casselman moved slowly away from the fire.

"Can't be!" Shain was awake. "We heard—"

"Shut up!" Casselman turned on him in a fury.

"I know what you heard," Danny said quietly. "You heard I wouldn't be with them this trip. Ever figure you might be double-crossed? That your partner might figure on warning the G of you to put himself in solid?"

Nobody said anything, and after a minute Casselman picked up a couple of sticks and tossed them on the fire. Shain stared at him, then at Papago Brown. "I'm going to sleep," he said, and added significantly, "and I mean *sleep!*"

"I reckon," Short said quietly, "that's a good idea. For all of us."

Nobody said anything for several minutes, while the girl lay breathless, feeling the tension in the room. The fire crackled and a stick fell, sending up a thin column of sparks. A wrong move could turn this room into red-laced hell from which none of them might emerge alive. Both Brown and Casselman knew that, for it would be point-blank shooting here.

Casselman sat down abruptly and began to pull off his boots. "I reckon," he said, "rest is the first thing."

Twice during the night Danny dozed lightly, but he was back in the shadows, and a watcher could not have told whether he dozed or whether the eyes were watchful from under his hat's low brim.

It was scarcely gray in the east when he touched her boot. Like a wraith he moved beside the bunk. "Come!" he whispered, and she followed him.

After the stuffy air of the tightly closed room the morning was like wine in her lungs. The rain had broken, and there were scattered clouds with fire along their edges in the east. Swiftly, he saddled their horses and they took the trail.

Several times she glanced at him. "Did somebody speak of Lonigan last night? I thought I heard the name."

"Could be," he said, with the flush of the rising sun on his face. "I've heard the name, and I reckon," he smiled a little, "they had heard it too!"

The drum of hoofs on the turf warned them and they looked up to see Calkins and Laredo Lee riding toward them. They drew up sharply when they saw she was not alone, and she had the feeling that Danny made some sharp signal from behind her back. "You all right?" Calkins demanded abruptly. "We was some worried."

"All right," she said. "This is Danny. He knows the Circle G."

"Yeah, I remember him," Calkins said. "Laredo, you ride on ahead with the boss. I want to make talk with Danny."

When they were well ahead, Calkins turned on him. "You son of a gun! Where you been? We need you the worst way."

"Not so bad as you will," Danny replied, and then went on to tell of the riders in the cabin. "And there'd been others there before them. When we came up I saw the tracks of maybe six or eight riders."

"She know who you are?"

Danny shook his head. "Doubt it. My name was mentioned last night, but I don't believe she quite got it. Not that it matters. Hoey will know me."

"He might not. You've changed, Lonigan. Changed a sight since he saw you. He was gone east, you know, an' you filled out a good bit, and you are some taller, too. Then . . . well, there's a different look about you. He might not be sure."

The herd came in sight and they drew up on the brow of the hill, looking down at them. "Reckon he knowed about that grass and water?" Calkins asked.

"He knew. He scouted it a couple of days ago. I spotted the herd quite a ways back, and when I saw what trail they were takin' I hung back, curious. Then I saw the old man wasn't with you and a girl was. So I waited, sizing up the layout."

"You figure he aims to steal the herd?"

"No . . . to buy it cheap. To get her scared of goin' broke, then making her an offer. He won't steal it unless all else fails. But chances are he'd steal the money back if he did buy it. He's deliberately kept this herd on the used-up trails to wear 'em down and scare her into a quick sale."

The herd pushed on into the brightening day, and Lonigan kept always on the far side of the herd from Hoey Ives. Calkins, riding near Ruth, warned her to say nothing of the new rider to Hoey. She glanced at him, and her chin lifted resentfully. Then she pulled on ahead.

Still, she was worried. What had the strange riders been doing in that cabin? Wasn't what she had heard true? That riders loitering in this area without herds were suspect? And that bunch! She was well aware that only the presence of the mysterious Danny had prevented trouble, and some curious understanding there was between Danny and those men. Could they be working together? Could all of that have been an elaborate pretense to get him with the herd?

\*      \*      \*

Hoey cantered his horse up to her and glanced at her sharply. "You all right? I was off looking in the other direction and just got back. We were all worried."

"I'm all right. Hoey," she asked suddenly, "why are we following this route? Why don't we go west to that valley? There's grass there."

He seemed astonished. "Grass? There is? I can't believe it! The last time I came over this trail it was a canyon of dust." He paused, then said, "If there's grass, of course we'll go. I'll turn the herd."

"Wait." She hesitated, then shook away her doubts. "Hoey, we've a new rider."

"What?" He drew up, his face stiff. "Where'd you get him?"

"I met him last night. There were some men in the cabin where we took shelter. He seemed to know them. A man named Casselman and one called Papago Brown."

"This rider knew them?" He seemed relieved, and Ruth watched him, puzzled and doubtful. "He's probably a good hand. I'll talk to him later. We can use the help."

The clouds did not leave, but hung low, bulging, and ominous. Yet it was not cool, but sultry with heat. Ruth kept again to the crests, yet was glad when the first of the herd spilled over into the canyon and headed for the thin trickle of the stream. They waded into it, scattering along the stream for three quarters of a mile, drinking, then moving out to crop the green grass.

Calkins rode up to her. "Why not bed down here?" he asked. "Let 'em get their fill? They'll drive easier tomorrow."

She moved back toward the chuck wagon and saw Laredo Lee already there, watching the cook make coffee. He looked up at her, a thin, sandy man with large freckles and cool blue eyes. He had been riding for the Circle G for three years and made the last drive with her father. "I hear you aim to make Ives foreman," he said, glancing at her. "If you do, why figure to hire a man to take my place."

"I'd be sorry to lose you, Laredo," she said sincerely. Then she turned on him. "Well, who would you want for foreman?"

He grinned. "Why, this new man. Danny would do. The boys like him."

"Oh, no! Not him!" She accepted a cup of coffee and watched Hoey come riding up to the fire. He looked angry and he swung down from the saddle; then he walked over to her.

"Look," he said, "finding this grass an' water is a break, but I happen to know there isn't much of it. You are only halfway to Dodge and have rough country and trouble ahead. There's no need to make this drive. I'll buy your herd."

"You?" she was startled. "Why?" She looked up at him, puzzled. "For how much?"

"Four dollars a head. Right here and now. In cash."

*"Four dollars?"* She shook her head. "That's ridiculous! They will bring five times that in Dodge."

"If they are fat. If they get there. But what if you lose three or four hundred head?"

Laredo Lee stood silent, watching Ruth with keen eyes. He wanted to speak, but was wise enough to know it was not the time. This was Ruth Gurney's problem. A moment later Lee was stifling his grin in the coffee cup.

"No, Hoey," she replied calmly, "I'll not quit now. These cattle started for Dodge and they will go to Dodge. My father never quit a trail drive in his life, and I won't."

Ives's face hardened and grew impatient. "Ruth, you don't know what you're gettin' into! Why, we haven't hit the hard part yet! There's Kiowas and Comanches up ahead, and that's to say nothin' of the rustlers."

"Boss," Lee spoke softly, "Mr. Ives ain't been over

a trail with the G afore. He don't know how we are."
The blue eyes were deceptively mild now as they looked
at Hoey. "The G," he explained, "figures it's plumb
salty. Why, we welcome a little brush with Indians. As
for rustlers, we eat 'em up! The old man," he added
affectionately, "liked a good fight. Last couple of drives
he put most of that on Lonigan's shoulders."

"Well," Ives snapped, "Lonigan ain't here now! If
he was," he sneered so openly that Ruth looked at him
in surprise, "he couldn't do much!"

"Maybe," a new voice said, "you're right. Again,
maybe you're not."

All turned. Calkins had come up, and several of
the other hands, but it was Danny Lonigan who spoke.
He stood alone in the middle of a little open space near
the wagon, a tall young man, narrow in the hips and
wide in the shoulder. He stood with his boots together,
one knee slightly bent, his hands busied with rolling a
cigarette.

Hoey Ives stared. Slowly, doubt, dismay, and uncertainty colored his features. "Who're you?" he demanded.

"Why, you remember me, Hoey," Lonigan said
quietly, "I whupped the socks off you one time at a
dance. That was afore you went away. You were trailin'
with that big Casselman then, an' figured it made you
some tough. You'll recall it didn't help you none."

Ives's lips tightened and his eyes grew cold. "So
you came back, did you? Well, I'm the boss here now.
You work for the G, you work for me."

"No," Lonigan said quietly, "I work for the lady
boss. She's the Circle G, Ives, and from the way she
stopped you on that offer to buy her out, I reckon she'll
do to ride the river with. The old man," he said,
"evidently bred true. I'll ride for her, Ives. Not for
you."

"I reckon that speaks my piece," Laredo Lee inter-
posed quietly.

"And mine," Calkins said.

Hoey Ives's face flushed. Then he laughed, "Well, that's fine! I wanted to be rid of you! I've got a bunch of boys ready to take over, and I'll have them in here by sundown. You boys can pack your duffle and hit the trail."

"No."

Ruth Gurney spoke in a clear, definite voice. All eyes turned to her. "Calkins told me something the other day that I've been thinking of. He said it was the hands that made the brand, the men who fought for it, worked for it, bled for it. They had a stake in the brand, and it was something above and beyond ownership. I believe that.

"Hoey, I'm sorry. You'll have to step out of your job. I want you with us, but not in charge of the work. I've made my decision and I'll abide by it." She turned her head. "Calkins, you take over. You're the foreman for the rest of the drive."

"But . . . ?" Calkins started to protest when Lonigan cut him short.

"Take it," he said briefly. "Let's move!"

"All right," Calkins said, pointing, "roll the wagon into that hollow under the cliff. We'll bed down here and roll 'em up the trail tomorrow."

Hoey Ives turned abruptly and stalked angrily away. Ruth took a step as though to follow, then turned back to the wagon. Her eyes met those of Lonigan. "Why didn't you tell me who you were?" she demanded impatiently. "I'd heard of you."

"What could I have said?" he shrugged. "Anyway, I'm with the drive again, and workin' with the G." He glanced at her quizzically. "Or am I?"

"Ask Calkins," she returned sharply. "He does the hiring!"

Throughout the day she saw no more of Ives, although she knew he was about. The hands rested when

they were not riding herd, all but Danny Lonigan. He
cleaned his guns carefully, then his rifle. After that he
went to work and repaired a wooden bucket that had
been broken a day before, and mended a halter. Several times he mounted and rode up to the rim of the
canyon and sat there, studying the country.

Calkins stopped by her seat just before sundown.
"What do you think, Calkins? Will we get the herd
through?"

He hesitated, then nodded slowly. "I wouldn't want
to get your hopes up, but I think so. Maybe this grass
won't hold, but we'll chance it, although come rain
we'd have to get to high ground. If there's much of this
grass, we'll make it, all right. But it will be a tough
squeeze and you won't make much money."

Lonigan walked slowly over to them, and as he
drew near, he removed his sombrero. "Ma'am," he
said, "I couldn't but overhear what was said. If . . . if
you'll let me make a suggestion . . ."

"I hope," Ruth said with dignity, "that I am always
open to suggestions. Yes, you may. What is it?"

"Why, just don't sell your herd atall!" he said
calmly. "Hang onto it. You're gettin' to Dodge at the
bad end of the season; prices will be down and your
herd in plumb bad shape. I'd say, hold your cows until
next spring, hold 'em on Nebraska grass, then fetch 'em
back to market, fat as ticks."

Ruth Gurney shook her head. "It is a good suggestion," she admitted, "but I can't. Until I sell this herd I
can't pay any of you. And I owe mortgage on the
ranch."

Lonigan shook his head. "Nuh-uh. Ma'am, I know
an hombre in Dodge who knows a good deal when he
sees it. He'll advance the money and take a mortgage
on your herd. You can pay up when you sell out. You'll
have fat stock and the first market in the spring. Believe me, you'll get twice what you could get with a
good herd now, let alone this scrawny lot. And you'll
have calves," he added.

"Excellent idea," Hoey Ives said quietly. He had come up unobserved. "In fact, that was what I planned to do . . . and what I'll still do."

Four men were ranged behind him, four men with rifles. Two more stood by the wagon, facing toward the herd. While the riders had watched for horsemen they had slipped up on foot, working their way through the brush like Indians.

Lonigan's eyes went to the rifles, then the riflemen. "You're tryin' to get yourself killed, Hoey. Now take your boys and light a shuck."

Ives chuckled. "Oh, no! We've got our herd. When your boys hear us call, they'll come in. They'll never know what hit 'em!"

"You mean," Danny Lonigan's voice was casual, "like this?" His hands flashed for his guns, and for one startled instant, every man froze. Then as one person, Ruth dropped to the ground and Ives, Calkins, and Lee grabbed iron.

It was Lonigan's sudden move that decided it. His first two shots knocked Casselman staggering and his third dropped Shain dead in his tracks. "Drop it, Short!" Lonigan yelled, and switched both guns to Papago Brown.

Then, suddenly, it was all over and where the cannonade of guns had sounded there was stillness, and somewhere down the valley, a quail called plaintively in the late dusk. Gunpowder left an acrid smell that mingled with the wood smoke of the freshly built fire.

Danny Lonigan looked down at Hoey Ives. Caught in the crossfire of Calkins's and Lee's guns, he had been riddled with bullets before he could more than fire his first shot.

Ruth, lying on her face, had a rifle on the two startled men near the wagon. The cook held an old muzzle-loading Civil War rifle on them, too.

Calkins swore softly. "You oughta give a man

warnin', Lonigan," he objected. "That was too sudden. They might have got us all!"

"Nuh-uh," Lonigan said quietly. "You see, I noticed that they were depending on the warning of the rifles. They didn't really expect anybody to take a chance. You see," he grinned grimly, "I noticed that none of their rifles were cocked! I knew I could get off several shots before they could cock and aim again."

"Yeah," Laredo said, "and what about Ives? What did you think he'd be doin'?"

"What he is doin'," Lonigan said quietly. "You see, I've rode the trail with you hombres before. Nobody needed to tell me what would happen. I knew."

He turned his head and looked at Olin Short. "You," he said, "would have sided me to help Miss Gurney in the cabin that night. I didn't want to kill you. Get your horse and slope. Take those others with you. And don't let 'em cross the trail again. As for you, Short, at heart you're too good a man for an outlaw. If you're down in Texas, stop by the G."

When he was gone, Lonigan turned to Ruth, who had got shakily to her feet, keeping her eyes averted from the fallen men. Taking her arm, he led her away from them, and away from the fire.

"We'll do what you said," Ruth said finally. "We'll drive to Nebraska and feed the stock there. Would you," she hesitated, "would you consider the foreman's job? I mean, in Calkins's place?"

"Why, no, I wouldn't." She turned toward him, half in surprise, half in regret. "No, I like Calkins, and he'll make a good foreman. The men like him, too. Besides, I've other plans."

"Oh." The word sounded empty and alone. "I . . . I hoped we'd see more of each other. You see, Dad . . ."

"We'll see more of each other, a lot more. When you put Hoey out as foreman and Calkins in, and again when you hit ground and grabbed that rifle, you showed what I said was right, that the old man bred true. You got what he had. You've nerve; you've iron in you. It's a line that should be carried on, so I'm not goin' to be your foreman. *I'm goin' to marry you.*"

She blinked.

"*Just like that?* Without any . . ."

"Courtin'?" He grinned. "Ma'am, there's no preacher this side of Dodge. Believe me, by the time you get there you'll be well courted, or my name ain't Lonigan!"

"Don't I get a chance to say yes or no?" she protested.

"You can say yes," he said, "if you say it fast, but for the next thirty minutes you're goin' to be busy." He put her chin up and his arm around her. "*Mighty busy,*" he said softly.

Somewhere down the valley a quail called plaintively into the darkness, and the stream chuckled over the stones. It probably had considerable to chuckle about.

# AUTHOR'S NOTE
# THE BUNKHOUSE

*In the earliest days ranch buildings were apt to be whatever could be thrown together in a hurry, and they often looked it. Corrals were usually made of poles cut from the nearest trees, often those growing along some nearby creek. Later, when time and money permitted, the ranch house was enlarged and often a bunkhouse was built to accommodate the regular hands, which might number from two to twenty, depending on the size of the ranch and the season. At round-up time there was a demand for additional help.*

*There would be rows of bunks, usually two-tiered, along the wall or walls, a table, and some benches or chairs. Depending on when and where the bunkhouse was built, it might have a fireplace or a potbellied stove, and also depending on where the ranch was, there might be an outside mirror and a small stand for a water bucket and basin. Nearby would hang a roller towel.*

*Depending on the nature and upbringing of the cowboys, the bunkhouse might be neat or untidy, but there was often a former soldier or sailor who, due to training, kept his possessions in one place and his bunk made up. There was also apt to be old coats hanging from pegs or nails along the walls, coal-oil lamps with reflectors, a worn pack of cards and perhaps a checkerboard and dominoes for entertainment, when there was time for it. Bedding was usually furnished by the ranch, but a good many drifting cow punchers carried their own. Most bunkhouses were simply places to sleep, but cowboys often added their own ideas of decoration to make them more homelike.*

*Owners and cowhands ate at the same table on most ranches, and there was little conversation. Eating was a serious business, and the hands usually washed up, slicked down their hair, and headed for the table. Once the meal was finished, they went back to the bunkhouse to sleep, or perhaps for some talk around the corral.*

*The larger the ranch, in most cases, the greater the distance between the owner or superintendent and the working hands. On many ranches the wife of the boss— and his daughters, if he had any—put the food on the table and often cooked the meals.*

*These practices varied widely, depending on the situation and the attitude of the owner and his family. On the larger ranches a cowhand might never see the inside of the big house, nor did he particularly wish to. The cowboy had his own pride and did not wish to intrude or be intruded upon. Although he might have only a "ten dollar horse and a forty dollar saddle," the idea that he might not be the equal of any man never entered his head, and if there were any doubt about it, he could always get up on his horse and ride off into the sunset.*

*Young people being what they are, there no doubt were cases when a cowhand married the boss's daughter. But then, as now, the boss was usually looking for an advantageous marriage for his daughter and a drifting cowhand was not likely to be among those considered. If there was not a likely young man on a nearby ranch, there was always the chance of meeting one after cattle sales in Kansas City or Denver, where wealthy cattlemen often congregated to relax away from the ranch. The Brown Palace Hotel in Denver was for many years just such a mecca for cattlemen and their families.*

# Regan of the Slash B

Dan Regan came up to the stage station at sundown and glanced quickly toward the window to see if the girl was there. She was. He stripped the saddle from his horse and rubbed the animal down with a handful of hay. Lew Meadows came down from the house and watched him silently.

"You don't often get over this way," Meadows said, pointedly.

Dan Regan paused from his work and straightened, resting a hand on the sorrel's withers. "Not often," he said. "I keep busy in the hills."

Meadows was curious and a little worried. Dan Regan was a lion hunter for the big Slash B outfit, but he was a newcomer to the country, and nothing much was known about him. There were too many men around the country now, too many that were new. Tough men, with hard jaws and careful eyes. He knew the look of them, and did not like what that look implied.

"Seen any riders up your way?"

Regan had gone back to working on the sorrel. He accepted the question and thought about it. "Not many," he said, at last. "A few strangers."

29

"They've been coming here, too. There's a couple of them inside now. Burr Fulton and Bill Hefferman."

Dan Regan slapped the sorrel on the hip and wiped his hands. "I've heard of them. They used to waste around down to Weaver."

"Having a daughter like mine is a bad thing out here," Meadows told him, the worry plain in his voice. "These men worry me."

"She looks fit to hold her own," Dan commented mildly.

Meadows looked at him. "You don't know Fulton. He's a lawless man; so are they all. They know what's happening. The word's gone out."

"What word?" Dan asked sharply.

Meadows shrugged. "Can't you see? The Slash B runs this country, always has. The Slash B was the law. Before Billings's time this was outlaw country, wild and rough, and the outlaws did what they wanted. Then Cash Billings came in and made law where there was none. He had an outfit of hardcase riders and when anybody overstepped what Billings thought was proper, the man was shot, or ordered out of the country. They made a few mistakes, but they had order. It was safe."

"The country's building up now. There's a sheriff."

Meadows spat his disgust. "Bah! Colmer's afraid of his shadow. Fulton ordered him out of the saloon over at the Crossing the other night and he went like a whipped dog."

"What about the Slash B? Has it lost its authority?"

"You don't hear much, up there in the hills. The Slash B is through, finished. Cash is a sick man, and that nephew of his is a weakling. The foreman is drunk half the time, and the old crowd is drifting away. That's why the wolves are coming. They know there's no bull moose for this herd. They want to start cutting it for their own profit."

Meadows nodded toward the house. "Where do Fulton and Hefferman get their money? They spend it free enough, but never do a pat of work. They sell Slash B cows, that's how. I wish somebody could talk to Cash. He doesn't know. He lives alone in that big house, and he hears nothing but what they tell him."

Meadows walked off toward the house and Dan Regan stood there in the darkening barn and brushed off his clothes. This was not quite new to him. He had known some of it, but not that it had grown so bad. Maybe if he went to Cash Billings . . . No, that would never do. Cash knew he had a lion hunter, but he didn't know he was Dan Regan, which was just as well.

Regan was a lean young man, as accustomed to walking as riding. He understood the woods and trails, knew cattle and lions. He was killing a lot of the latter. He walked on up to the house and into the big dining room where they fed the stage passengers and any chance travelers following the route. The table was empty except for a fat-faced drummer with a wing collar, and the two riders Lew Meadows had mentioned.

Burr Fulton was a lean whip of a man, as tall as Regan but not so broad. Hefferman was beefy, a heavy-shouldered man with thick-lidded eyes and a wide, almost flat, red face. He looked as tough and brutal as Regan knew him to be. Neither of them looked up to see who had entered. They did not care. They were men riding a good thing, and they knew it.

Dan Regan had seen this thing happen before. He had seen big outfits lose their power. He had seen the wolves cut in and rip the herds to bits, taunting the impotent outfit that had once wielded power, and rustling its herds without retaliation. It was always the big herds, the strong outfits, that went down the hardest.

He seated himself on the bench some distance away from the others, and after a minute Jenny Meadows came in and brought his dinner. He glanced up and their eyes met quickly, and Jenny looked hastily away, a little color coming into her cheeks.

It had been a month since she had seen this man, but she hadn't forgotten a thing about him, remembering the lean strength of his face, the way his dark hair curled behind his ears, and the way his broad shoulders swelled the flannel of his shirt.

She put his food down, then hesitated. "Coffee?"

"Milk, if you've got it. I never get any up in the mountains."

Hefferman heard the word and glanced over at him.

"Milk," he said to Fulton. "He drinks milk."

Burr laughed. "He's from the Slash B. I think they all drink milk these days!"

Regan felt his ears burning and some dark, uneasy warmth stirring in his chest. He did not look up, but continued to eat. Meadows was standing in the door and overheard Fulton's comment. Now he sat down across the table from Regan and poured a cup of coffee.

"Meadows," Fulton said, looking up, "do you use Slash B beef? Best around here, and I hear it can be had cheap."

"I have my own cows," Meadows replied stiffly. He was a somber man, gray haired and thin. Never a fighter, he had a stern, unyielding sense of justice and a willingness to battle if pushed. He had lived safely here, in the shadow of the Slash B.

"Might as well buy some of their beef," Hefferman boomed. "Everybody else is!"

Jenny returned and put a glass of milk in front of Regan. Her own face was burning, for the remarks had been audible in the kitchen, and she knew they were deliberately trying to make trouble. It irritated her that Regan took no offense and she was ashamed for him.

Moreover, she was sure that Dan Regan had come to the stage station to see her. Remembering the impression he had made the first time, she also remembered his eyes on her, and how they had made her feel. He was, she knew, the first man who had awakened within her the sense of being female, of being a woman. It was a new sensation, and an exciting one.

The supplies he had bought on his last trip were enough for another month at least, yet he had come back now. Knowing he came to see her, and remembering the excitement he had roused in her on his last trip, she regarded him somewhat as her own. It displeased her to see him sit quietly before the taunts of the two badlands riders.

Meadows was thinking similar thoughts. Jenny worried him. It was bad enough to have a daughter to rear on the frontier, worse when she had no mother. He hated to think of her leaving him, yet he knew when she married it would be a distinct relief. His ideas on women were strict, dogmatic, and old-fashioned, yet he was aware that nature takes little note of the rules of men. Still, the malpais country offered little in the way of eligible males.

He was aware of the dark good looks of Burr Fulton, and that such a man might appear dashing and exciting to a girl like Jenny. Dan Regan's first visit to the stage station had arrested his notice as it had Jenny's, for here was a tall, fine-looking man with a steady way about him and a good job, even if it was with the declining Slash B.

Meadows wanted no trouble around his place, and yet, like Jenny, he was irritated that Regan took no offense at the ragging Fulton and Hefferman were giving him.

Burr looked up suddenly at Jenny.

"Dance over to Rock Springs next week. Want to ride over with me?"

"No," Jenny replied, "I don't want to ride anywhere with a man who makes a living by stealing other men's beef!"

Fulton's face flushed with angry blood and he half rose to his feet. "If you were a man," he said, "I'd kill you for that!" He remained hard. "Might as well come," he said. "You'll at least be going with a man who could protect you. I don't drink milk!"

"It might be better if you did!" she retorted.

After a few minutes, with a few more sarcastic remarks, the two got up and went outside, mounted, and rode away. After they were gone the silence was thick in the room. Dan Regan stared gloomily at his milk, aware of Meadows's irritation and Jenny's obvious displeasure.

He looked up, finally. "That was what I came down for, Jenny. I want to take you to that dance."

She turned on him, and her face was stiff. Her chin lifted. "I'd not want to go with you," she said bitterly. "You'd be afraid to stand up for a girl! You won't even stand up for your own rights! I thought you were a *man!*"

The moment the angry words were out, she would have given anything not to have said them. She hesitated, instantly contrite. Dan Regan took one more swallow of milk and got up. Coolly, but with his face pale and his eyes grim, he picked up his hat.

"I reckon that settles that," he said quietly, "and I'll be riding on."

Jenny took an impulsive step toward him, not finding the words to stop him, but his back was turned. Only at the door did he turn.

"What did you want?" he asked coldly. "A killing? for so little? Is a man's life so small a thing to you?"

She stared at the door, appalled. Then her eyes went to her father's.

"But, Dad! He—it wouldn't have meant a killing!"

Meadows looked up, realization in his eyes. "It might, Jenny. It might, at that."

It was young Tom Newton who took her to the dance. A handsome boy he was, a year younger than she, and a rider for the Slash Bar. Yet the moment she walked through the door of the Rock Springs school she sensed the subtle difference in the atmosphere. The same people were there, but now a queer restraint seemed to sit upon them. The reason was not hard to see. Burr Fulton was there, with Bill Hefferman and some dozen other hardcase riders, all outside men, all tough, and all drinking.

Yet the affair started well, and it was not until after three dances that she glanced toward the door and saw Dan Regan. There was a subtle difference about him, too, and for a moment she could not place it, and then she saw. He was wearing two guns. It was the first time she had ever seen him with anything but a rifle, yet he wore the guns naturally, easily.

He wore a dark broadcloth suit that somehow suited him better than she would have believed. He did not wear it with the stiff, dressed-up manner of most western men, but with the ease of one long accustomed to such clothes. The change was good, she decided, for he managed to look not only perfectly at ease, but completely the gentleman.

As the evening wore on, the Fulton riders grew more boisterous. Hefferman walked out on the floor and took a girl from another man by the simple procedure of shoving the man away. White-faced, the girl danced with him, and when the dance was over, she and her friend left. Others began to drift away, and somberly, Dan Regan watched them go.

Jenny Meadows was perfectly aware it was time she left, but Dan had made no effort to come to her, nor to request a dance. Disappointed, and more than a little angry, she delayed even after Tom Newton began to urge her to leave with him.

Once, early in the evening, she had danced with Burr Fulton. He had teased her a little, but his behavior had been all she could have asked. Now he came to her again, his face flushed with drinking.

"Let's dance!" he said, grinning at her.

She was frightened at the lurking deviltry in his

eyes, and she could see the temper riding him. Fulton was a reckless man, a man known to be ugly when drinking—and dangerous. She hesitated, and Newton spoke up quietly. "She has this dance with me, Burr."

Fulton stared insolently at Newton, and Jenny felt a rising sense of panic.

"You mean she did!" he said. "She has this dance with me, now!"

Newton's face paled, but he stood his ground. "I'm sorry, Burr. She dances with me this time. Another time, perhaps."

"This time." Burr Fulton's attention was centered on Newton now. "This time she dances with me. You take a walk or get your horse and ride home. I'll take care of her!"

She turned quickly to Newton. "We'd better go, Tom. We should have gone long ago."

Fulton's eyes turned to her then, and the taunting violence in them shocked her. "You stay until I get through with you!" he said. "Maybe I'll take you home tomorrow!"

Tom Newton's fist swung. It was a nice try, but Burr had been looking for it, hoping for it. He knocked the punch down and kicked Newton in the stomach. With a grunt, the boy fell to the floor, his face twisted with pain.

Suddenly Dan Regan had stepped between Jenny and Fulton. "That was a dirty trick, Burr," said Regan. "You didn't have to kick him. Now you and your boys had better go home, you're spoiling a good dance, and insulting women."

Fulton's face tightened. "Why, you lily-livered skunk, I'll kill—!"

The words stopped, for he was looking into a six-gun, and then he realized that the gun had been in Dan Regan's hands.

"So? A sure-thing operator, aren't you?" he sneered.

"Walk up to a man with a gun in your hand! Don't take no chances, do you? Holster that gun and give me a fair shake! I'll kill you then! I'll shoot you like a dog!"

"You talk too much!" Regan said, disgust in his voice. "Take your coyote pack and trail out of here. Move now!"

His eyes ugly, Fulton turned his back on Dan and walked away. The dance broke up quietly. Regan stood alone and watched them go. Nobody came near him, nobody spoke to him, not even Jenny Meadows. Bitterly, he watched them go, knowing in his heart how they felt. He was afraid to give a man an even break, he came up with the drop on Fulton . . . he wouldn't take a chance.

All of them were glad that Fulton had been stopped before something more ugly happened, but this was not the way of the west. You faced a man, and you gave him an even break.

Dan Regan did not stop at the stage station on his way back to the hills. He just kept going until the high timber closed around him and his sorrel was soft-footing it over thick pine needles toward the cabin on the bench above Hidden Lake.

"We'd better forget her, Red," he told the sorrel. "She thinks we're yellow. And so do the rest of them."

Rumors came to him by occasional passing prospectors or hunters. Rustlers were harrying the Slash B by day and by night. The herds were decimated. Two of the Slash B riders had been shot. When the foreman had threatened reprisals, Burr Fulton had ridden right up to the Slash B bunkhouse, dragged the man from his bunk, and whipped him soundly. When the punchers had wanted to round up the gang, their frightened foreman had refused permission. What had begun as a series of raids on the Slash B had grown until almost a reign of terror existed in the malpais.

Three of the hands quit. Drifting out of the country, they stopped at Regan's cabin.

"Had enough!" Curly Bowne said with disgust. "I never worked for a white-feathered outfit, and I never will! If they'd turned us loose we could have cleaned out that bunch, but young Bud Billings is afraid of his shadow. The old man is sick, and Anse Wiley, the foreman, is plenty buffaloed now."

"Stick around," Regan told them. "No use you boys riding out of the country. There's plenty of grub here, and you can hole up and help me hunt lions for a few days. I've been sort of thinking about going down to talk to old Cash, myself."

Webb looked at him cynically. "Heard you had a run-in with Burr," he suggested.

Curly Bowne and Jim Webb studied their boot toes. Dan knew they were awaiting his reply. These men had always liked him, but nobody in the malpais knew much about Regan. He was just the Slash B lion hunter. The story they had heard about the dance did not show him up too well.

"I had a few words with him," Regan said calmly. "He dared me to holster my gun, said he'd kill me if I gave him an even break."

"You didn't do it?"

"No." Regan's voice was flat. "I've no use for killing unless forced to it, and there were women and old folks around. Anyway it wouldn't have been an even break for Burr. He never saw the day he could throw a gun with me."

He said it so calmly, in such a completely matter-of-fact tone that it didn't sound like boasting. Curly looked at him thoughtfully.

"Why don't you go down and see the old man?" he suggested then. "We'll hold on here for you."

Dan Regan rode by way of the stage station trail and arrived there at sundown once more. Jenny was putting food on the table when he went in, and her father glanced up at him.

"Howdy, Dan," Meadows said grimly. "Reckon you can say good-bye to us now. We're leaving!"

Regan twisted his hat in his fingers, avoiding Jenny's eyes.

"Scared out?" he asked.

Jenny's old irritation with him surfaced once more.

"If I were you I'd not talk about being scared!" she said scornfully.

He glanced at her without expression. "All right," he said quietly.

"Or anything else!" she flashed.

"Did I say I was?" he asked gently.

Her face flamed and she whipped around and walked from the room, her chin high.

"Jenny's sort of upset lately," Meadows commented. "Don't seem like herself."

"Burr been around?"

"Every night. That Bill Hefferman, too. He's a mean one, he is."

"I'll be ridin' on, I reckon," Dan said. "Got to go over to the Slash B."

"Drawin' your time? They all quittin'?"

"No," Dan Regan said quietly. "I'm applying for a job. I want Anse Wiley's job—ramroddin' the Slash B."

Meadows stared. "You're crazy!" he said. "Plumb crazy! That outfit would run you out of the country or kill you! Burr Fulton has Wiley so buffaloed he doesn't know which end is up!"

The door slammed open and Bill Hefferman came in. "Coffee!" he roared. "Give me some coffee!" He grabbed Meadows by the collar and shoved him toward the kitchen just as Jenny appeared in the door, her eyes wide and startled. "Get me some coffee!"

"You make too much noise," Regan said, looking up at him. He sat on a seat against the wall, his arms folded.

Hefferman turned his big head and stared. He was a giant of a man. When he saw who it was he sneered.

"You? Don't even open your yap at me, cat hunter! I don't like you, and I'd like nothing better than to smash your face in!"

"Get out," Regan said, unmoving. "Get out and don't come back until tomorrow afternoon. I'll meet you here then, and if you want trouble, I'll whip you—bare-handed!"

"What?" Hefferman spoke in a hoarse whisper. "You'd fight me with your hands?"

"Yes, and beat your head to jelly! Now get out of here!"

"Get out, is it?" Hefferman started for Regan. "I'll throw you out!"

He was walking fast, and Dan reached out with a toe of his boot and hooked a chair with it, kicking it into the bigger man's ankles. Hefferman ran into the chair in midstride and came down with a stunning crash. He drew back to his knees, clumsily kicking the ruins of the chair loose from his ankles. When he lifted his dazed eyes he was looking into Dan Regan's six-shooter.

"Beat it!" Dan said quietly. "You light a shuck!"

Slowly, his eyes clearing, Hefferman got to his feet. "I'll kill you for this!" he said viciously.

"All right. Tomorrow. With your fists," Regan said. "Don't be late. Three is the hour!"

When he was gone, Meadows shook his head. "You sure do beat all!" he said. "You get out of fixes better than any man I ever saw! But now you've got a chance to get away, and you better do it!"

"Leave?" Regan smiled. "And miss all the fun? Don't worry, I'll be here tomorrow! And while I think of it, you'd best not sell out if you haven't, nor plan on leaving. There's going to be a change around here!"

He walked out, leaving Jenny staring after him with puzzled eyes. "Dad, what's the matter with him? Is he afraid, or is he a fool?"

Meadows lit his pipe. "I don't know, Jenny darling," he said, "but I've a feeling he's neither!"

It was spitting snow when Dan Regan rode into the ranch yard of the Slash B. He walked his horse across the yard to the rail by the house, dismounted, and tied him. Then he started up the steps.

"Wait a minute!" It was Anse Wiley. "You can't go in there!"

"Who says I can't?"

"I do!"

"Then it doesn't mean a thing. Go on back to the bunkhouse out of this snow. I want to see Cash."

"Cash?" Wiley's face was angry. "He's a sick man. Nobody sees him!"

"That gag worked too long and too well for you and Bud," Regan said. "I know all about you. You've been stealing the place blind, both of you. Now the fun is over. Get out of town or get thrown in jail!"

The foreman stared at him, aghast.

"I'm not talking through my hat," Regan added. "I have facts and figures. You tell Bud, and you can have twenty-four hours' start. No more."

Deliberately, he turned on his heel and walked in. Bud Billings came out of his chair with a startled exclamation. Dan moved by him toward Cash's room. "Stop!" Bud demanded. "What do you mean breaking in here?"

Regan looked at him. "Bud Billings, you're a cheap little thief! Now get out and join Wiley and get going or I'll throw you out!"

Bud stared, swallowed, and stepped out of the way. Dan Regan walked by him and threw open the door where old Cash lay propped up on some pillows.

The fierce old eyes blazed at him. "Who in tarnation are you?"

"Not one of the thieves you have around you!" Regan flashed back. "While you lie there in that bed, your nephew, Bud, has been stealing you blind and Wiley helping him! Now the rustlers have started in and they are cuttin' your herds day and night!"

"What's that?" Billings roared. "Who the devil are you?"

"I'm Dan Regan, Pat Regan's son!" Dan said calmly. "I've been working for you as a lion hunter and watching them steal you out of house and home until I got sick and tired of it!

"You lying there in that bed! You aren't sick, you old catamount! You just ate too much and laid around too much! After a man's been in the saddle as long as you he's got to die in the saddle! You figured you were rich and let Bud and Wiley talk you into taking it easy!"

Coolly then, Regan recited the events of the past few months, the whipping of Wiley, the laughing at the Slash B, the stealing without even attempting cover. "Bud didn't dare raise hob about it because he was stealin' himself!" he added.

Cash stared at him, chewing the ends of his mustache. "What right have you got to be here?" he demanded. "Your Pa and I never did get along!"

"No, you sure didn't, you pig-headed old fraud!" Dan told him. "Pat Regan spent a lifetime pulling you out of holes, and he told me to keep an eye on you, and that's what I've done. Now make me your foreman so I can get things going around here!"

Cash Billings stared at him angrily, and then suddenly, his eyes began to twinkle.

"Be dehorned if you ain't the spittin' image of Pat!" he said. "Only bigger! You're some bigger! All right! You're the new foreman! Now go ahead and run the show until I get on my feet!"

"You," Dan pointed his finger, "be on your feet in the morning, understand?"

He turned to go, and Cash stopped him. "Dan? Is that your name? You ever handled cows? What you been doin'?" Billings stared at him suspiciously.

Dan Regan smiled. "Why, I punched cows a while, took three herds up the trail to Dodge and then Ogallala. After that I was a Texas Ranger for about four years."

He walked down to the bunkhouse and opened the door. Tom Newton sat disconsolately before the fire. He glanced up.

"Oh? It's you? Did you run Wiley off?"

"Uh-huh. I'm the new foreman. Tom, you straddle your bronc and hightail it for my cabin. Curly Bowne, Jim Webb, and Jones are holed up there. Get them back down here but fast. Tell them I want them at the stage station, and you too, tomorrow not later than three."

"What happens then?" Tom asked, staring at this new Regan.

Dan smiled. "Why, first I'm going to lick the stuffing out of Bill Hefferman. Then I'm going to run Burr Fulton out of the country afoot and without pants! After that," he added grimly, "you and the rest of the boys are going to come with me. We're going to comb these brakes like they were never combed, and any man we find who doesn't start running when we see him will wear a hemp necktie or swallow lead! We're going to have this country fit to live in again!"

Bill Hefferman was sore. Moreover, he was boastful. He was a big man and a fighter, and there was no cowardly bone in all his huge body. Victor in many barroom and rangeland brawls, he feared no man and was confident he could whip anyone. Dan Regan he regarded as small potatoes. In fact, the entire Fulton crowd regarded it as a huge lark—if Dan showed up, and the betting was five to one he wouldn't.

One bettor was Jenny Meadows.

The Fulton crowd arrived early. Bottles had been passed around freely. Burr swaggered into the long dining room and dropped at the table to drink coffee and eat doughnuts, always available at the stage station.

"He'll be here!" Jenny said. Suddenly, though she could not have said why, she was very sure. "You wait and see!"

"Him?" Burr was incredulous. "He won't show up! Aside from Bill, I've got my own little score to pay off with him, and if he shows up, I aim to pay off!"

"He'll show up!" Jenny said firmly.

Burr grinned insolently. "Want to bet? I'll bet you a dollar he doesn't show!"

"Are you a piker?" Jenny flashed. "A dollar!" Scorn was thick in her voice. "What do you think I am, a child? I'll bet you one hundred dollars to five hundred! Those are the odds they are offering that he shows up. I'll bet you another hundred dollars to five hundred that when he shows up he will whip Bill Hefferman!"

Fulton stared, then laughed. "Are you crazy?" he demanded. "He hasn't a chance! If he had nerve enough he couldn't do it, and he's yellow as buttercups! Never gave anybody an even break!"

"I made my offer!" Jenny's face was pale, her eyes flashing. "Are you a piker? You've talked so big about the money you have! Put it up!"

He laughed, a little uneasily. He was unused to betting with a woman, and while he had no doubt he would win, still . . .

"He's yellow!" Burr persisted. "If he should whip Bill, which he won't, I'd run him out of the country!"

Thoroughly angry, Jenny said, "All right, then! If I win I'll bet all I win on the first two bets that *he* runs *you* out of the country!"

Burr Fulton sprang to his feet, white with anger.

"*Me?*" he roared. "Run *me* out? Why you lit—!" He broke off, staring at her. "All right," he said, "it's a bet!"

"Then let's put up our money!" Jenny said flatly. "If he runs you out of the country I'll have a hard time collecting! Here comes Dad and Colmer. We'll give the money to Dad to hold for us while Colmer is a witness!"

Burr slowly counted out the money, his face dark with anger and resentment. He felt that he had never been so insulted in his life. Secretly, he fancied himself another Billy the Kid, and this talk of running *him* out! He snorted.

As the hour hand straightened up to three o'clock, four riders came down the hill to the stage station and dismounted. Everyone there knew them—Tom Newton, Jim Webb, Curly Bowne, and Jack Jones. All were top hands, tough riders who had fought Indians and rustlers with the Slash B when Cash Billings was on his feet and ramrodding the spread himself. Lew Meadows eyed them thoughtfully, then stole a look at Burr. Fulton's face was a study in doubt and irritation.

Bill Hefferman peeled off his shirt and stepped out beyond the hitching rail. "Well, where is he?" he roared.

"Right here!" The reply was a ringing shout, and all heads turned. Dan Regan stood in the stable door. How he had gotten there or how long he had been there, nobody knew.

Jenny felt her heart give a great leap. He had come, then! He wasn't afraid!

Stripped to the waist, he looked a bigger man, and certainly a more rugged one, and powerfully muscled. He walked out and handed his shirt to Meadows. He wore two guns, tied low.

He stepped up to the mark Hefferman had drawn with a toe, and grinned at the big man.

"All right," he said cheerfully, "you asked for it!"

Both hands were carried chest high, rubbing the palms together, and as he spoke he smashed a straight left to Bill's mustache that staggered the big man and started a thin trickle of blood from his broken lips. Hefferman grunted and looped a roundhouse swing that missed. Dan Regan's left lanced that mustache three times, flashing like a striking snake. Then a right uppercut jerked the big man's head back, and the crowd roared.

Hefferman rushed, swinging. Regan parried one swing, ducked another, and caught the third on the chin going away, but went down hard. Bill rushed to get close and Dan rolled over and came to his feet. He stabbed another left to the mouth, took a smashing blow on the chin that rang bells in his head, and then he bored in, ripping wicked, short-arm punches to the body with all the drive of his powerful shoulders.

Bill pushed him away and swung with everything he had. The punch caught Regan on the chin, and he went down, turned a complete somersault, and lay stretched out on his face in the dust!

A shout went up from the Fulton men, and they began dancing around, slapping each other on the back. Then Regan got up.

They stared. Hefferman, astonished beyond reason, rushed. He met that same stiff left hand in the teeth, and it stopped him flat-footed. Before he could get untracked, Regan knocked him down with a right.

Lunging to his feet, Hefferman charged. The two began slugging like madmen. Bill grabbed Dan by the belt and shirt and heaved him high, but Dan jerked up with his knee and smashed Bill's nose to crumpled bone and flesh. Hefferman staggered and Regan broke loose. Dropping to his feet he set himself and threw two powerful swings to Bill's chin.

Like a lightning-shivered oak, the big man staggered and his knees buckled. Dan Regan walked in, threw a left, and then let go with a right to the belly that drove every bit of wind Hefferman had into one explosive grunt. The big man doubled, and Regan brought a right from his knees that lifted him from his feet and dropped him on his back in the dust!

He lay perfectly still.

Dan Regan stepped back quickly, working his fingers. His work-hardened hands felt good. Skinned on the knuckles, but still supple and quick.

"All right, Fulton!" he said.

Burr wheeled. The gunman dropped into a half crouch, his eyes suddenly aware. Triumph lit his eyes, and with a sneer, he dropped his hands.

Then he froze, still clutching the butts. He blinked and swallowed. He was looking into a pair of twin six-guns that had appeared in Dan Regan's hands as if by magic.

"It was a trick!" he roared. "A sneaking trick!"

Dan smiled. "Why, you tinhorn, try it again!"

He dropped his guns into his holsters and lifted his hands free. Before Burr Fulton could so much as tighten his grip on his own guns, Regan's had leaped from his holsters.

"Burr," Regan said quietly, "I told you you wouldn't have a chance with me! You're not a badman, you're just a wild-haired cowhand who got an idea he was fast! Back up and go to punching cows before you try to draw on the wrong man and get killed! You're no gun-slinger! You couldn't even carry a gunslinger's saddle!"

Burr Fulton swallowed. It was hard to take, but he was remembering the speed of those guns, noting the steadiness of them. "Try it again!" he screamed. "And come up shootin'! I'd rather be killed than made a fool of!" He was trembling with fury, his face white and strained.

"Burr," Dan replied patiently, "you're strictly small-time, and I'm not a scalp hunter. You draw on me and I'll shoot holes in your ears!"

Burr Fulton froze. Perhaps nothing else would have done it. *Holes in his ears!* The brand of a coward! Why, he would be ruined! He would . . . !

He stepped back and straightened up. "All right," he choked. "You win!"

"Now," Regan said. "I'm ramrodding the Slash B from here on! Anyone caught rustling our stock will be strung up right on the ranch and left hanging until he dries up and blows away! You've all got just until day-light to leave the country. Tomorrow my boys start combing the brakes, hunting for strangers. I hope we don't find any!"

Webb, Newton, Bowne, and Jones suddenly stepped

out in a solid rank. All four held double-barreled shot-guns which Curly had taken from their horses under cover of the fight.

"All right, boys! Start moving!" Dan said quietly. They moved.

Dan Regan walked up on the porch and looked at Jenny.

"Well, I'm back," he said, "and there's another dance at Rock Springs on Saturday. Want to go with your husband?"

"That's the only way I'll ever go to another dance there!" she replied tartly. "Anyway, we can buy furniture with the money."

"What money?" he asked suspiciously.

"The money I won from Burr Fulton, betting on you at five to one!" she said, smiling a little, her eyes very bright.

# AUTHOR'S NOTE
# THE WESTERN SALOONS

*Whiskey Flat, near where Kernville, California, now stands, began when a wagon broke down and the owner of the wagon and its goods began selling whiskey off the tailgate.*

*Parrot City, a now-vanished town not far from Durango, Colorado, began with a man who laid a plank across two barrel tops and began selling whiskey under a tree.*

*Saloons began wherever there was a market for whiskey, and that was wherever men congregated. The first saloons were often in tents, hastily thrown up while a building was in the process of construction. They were of all types, from a shed with a bar to a very plush and elaborate structure with gaslights, paintings (often of seminude, reclining ladies), and a stage for entertainment.*

*The saloon was not merely a place for drinking, but a clubhouse, information center, and meeting place, a place where deals were made for land, cattle, mining claims, or whatever.*

*Most of the saloons had gambling as well, the games run by the house or by someone working with permission from the house and an understanding. Many of the early peace officers were also gamblers, and on the frontier many gamblers were respected men.*

*The average western saloon was a place with a few gaming tables, sawdust on the floor, and a long bar. Whiskey was expensive to ship, and although a few bottles of the good stuff were handy for special customers or the owner himself, most of the patrons* were served whiskey or beer often concocted on the premises or nearby and made of whatever material was available.

By the time the railroads were operating in the west and whiskey could be shipped at a reasonable price, many westerners had forgotten what good whiskey tasted like and were convinced that so-called "Indian" whiskey was better.

Many western saloons also served meals, some even of gourmet quality, but on the whole such food was catch-as-catch-can, and one ate what was available and was glad to get it.

Women were rarely on the premises unless the saloon also functioned as a dance hall, in which case women appeared as entertainers, most with quarters upstairs to which they might resort on appeal. Occasionally the dance-hall girl would be only that, limiting her activities to dancing or talking with the customers. Others had special "friends" whom they might entertain on occasion or with whom they kept company, as the saying was.

As the railroad built west, the Hell-on-Wheels towns kept pace with construction, since workers on the railroad had to have a place to spend their money and these towns provided it. Most of the saloon and gambling houses at the end of the tracks were houses in tents, a few in hastily thrown up shacks. They were wild, woolly, and lawless, each "town" lasting for a few weeks only, then moving westward to be reestablished in a new location. Cheyenne, Wyoming, which practically began in that way, remained a permanent town, a marketing place, and eventually became an important city. Fortunately, in growing up, Cheyenne has managed to retain its western flavor, as befits a town in cattle country.

# Heritage of Hate

## Chapter 1
### *Bushwhacked Man*

Con Fargo hunched his buffalo coat about his ears and stared at the blood spot. It must have fallen only a minute or two before, or snow would have covered it. And the rapidly filling tracks beside the blood spot were those of a man.

Brushing the snow from his saddle he remounted, turning the grulla mustang down the arroyo. The man, whoever he might be, was wounded and afoot, and the worst storm in years was piling the ravines with drifts.

The direction of the tracks proved the man a stranger. No Black Rock man would head in that direction if badly hurt. In that direction lay thirty miles of desert, and at the end of those miles only the ramshackle ruins of a ghost town.

Con started the mustang off at a rapid trot, his eyes searching the snow. Suddenly, he glimpsed the wounded man. Yet even as his eyes found the stumbling figure, a shot rang out.

Fargo hit the trail beside his horse, six-gun in

hand. He could see nothing, only the blur of softly falling snow, hissing slightly. There was no sound, no movement. Then, just as he was about to avert his eyes, a clump of snow toppled from the lip of the arroyo.

He hesitated an instant, watching. Then he clambered up the steep wall of the arroyo and stood looking down at the tracks. Here a man had come to the edge, and here he had waited, kneeling in the snow. He was gone now, and within a quarter of a mile his tracks would be wiped out.

Con Fargo slid back into the arroyo and walked over to the fallen man. The fellow wore no heavy coat, and he was bleeding badly. Yet his heart was beating.

"This moving may cash your chips, old-timer, but you'd die out here, anyway," Con said.

He lifted the man and carried him back to his horse. It took some doing to get the wounded man into the saddle and mount behind him. The mustang didn't like the smell of blood and didn't like to carry double. When Fargo was in the saddle he let the grulla have his head, and the horse headed off through the storm, intent on the stable and an end to this foolishness.

An hour later, with the wounded man stripped of his clothes, Con went to work on him. He had the rough skill of the frontier fighter who was accustomed to working with wounds. The man had been shot twice. The first bullet had been high, just under his left collarbone, but it had spilled a lot of blood. The second shot had gone in right over the heart.

For three bitter days he fought for the man's life, three days of blizzard. Then the wounded man began to fail, and at daylight on the fourth morning, he died.

Getting out for a doctor would have been impossible. It was twelve miles to Black Rock, and with snow deep in the passes he dared not make the attempt. And the one doctor in town wouldn't cross the street to help Fargo or anyone like him.

Thoughtfully, Con studied the dead man. To some-body, somewhere, this man meant much. For whatever reason the man came west, it had been important enough to warrant his murder.

For this was no casual robbery and murder. Every effort had been made to prevent identification of the dead man. The labels had been torn from his store-bought clothes. There were no letters, no papers, no wallet and no money. All had been removed.

"Somebody went to a powerful lot of trouble to see nobody ever guessed who this hombre was," Con told himself. "I wonder why?"

The man was young, not over thirty. He was good-looking and had the face of a man with courage. Yet he was unburned by sun or wind, and his hands were soft.

Obviously, the killer thought the first shot had finished him. He had robbed the man and stripped the identification from his body, and then must have left him. The wounded man recovered consciousness and made an effort to get away. The killer had returned, had guessed the wounded man would keep to the par-tial shelter of the arroyo, and had headed him off and then shot him down.

"Pardner, I reckon I'm goin' to find out why," Con said softly. "You and me, they didn't want either of us here. You didn't have as much luck as I did. Or maybe you were slower on the draw."

Turning to a drawer in the table he got out a tape measure. Then, while frost thickened on the windows and the snow sifted down into drifts, he measured the body. The height, waist, chest, biceps. There was a small white scar on the dead man's chin; he noted it. On his right shoulder there was a birthmark, so Con put it down in the book.

"Somebody didn't want anybody to know who you was, so that must be important. Me, I aim to find out."

The next day, after he had buried the man in an old mine tunnel, he examined the clothing. One by one, in broad daylight, he went over the articles of clothing. There was red clay against the heels of both shoes, a stain of red clay around the edge of the sole.

On the seat of the trousers and the back of the coat were long gray hairs. "Either this hombre had him a furlined coat or he sat on a skin-covered seat. If a seat, that would most likely be a buckboard or wagon."

More red clay was found on the knees of the trousers. "Reckon this hombre fell onto his knees when shot," Con muttered. "Else a feller as neat as him would have brushed them off."

Red clay. There was a good bit of red clay near Massacre Rocks on the stage trail from Sulphur Springs.

"That mud was soft enough to stick," he said. "And that means he was shot when it wasn't froze none. Now that norther struck about noon the day I found him, so he must've been shot that morning."

An idea struck him suddenly. Bundling the clothes he put them in a sack and then in a box, which he hid in a hole under the floor. Then he slung his guns around his lean hips, donned his buffalo coat, slipped an extra gun into its spacious pocket, and picking up his rifle, went out to the stable.

The storm had broken about daybreak, so when the mustang was saddled he rode out taking the ridge trail, where the wind had kept thin the snow.

Two months earlier Con Fargo had ridden into Black Rock a total stranger. He came as heir to Tex Kilgore's range and property—and found he had inherited a bitter hatred from many, open dislike from others, and friendship nowhere.

Knowing Tex Kilgore he could understand some of it. Black Rock was a country of clans. It was close-knit, lawless, and suspicious and resentful of outsiders. Tex was bluff, outspoken, and what he believed he believed with everything in him. He was a broad-jawed, broad-shouldered man, and when he came into Black Rock he took up land nobody else had liked. Yet no sooner did he have it than others perceived its value. They tried to drive him out, and he fought back.

Being a fighting man, he fought well, and several men died. Then, aware that his time was running out, and that alone he could not win, he had written to Con Fargo:

> If you got the sand to fight for what's yourn, come a-runnin'.

Tex Kilgore knew his man, and half the money in the venture had been Con's money. Together they had punched cows for John Chisum. Together they had gone north to Dodge and Hay City with trail herds, and together they had been Texas Rangers.

Kilgore, older by ten years, had left to begin the ranch. Con Fargo stayed behind to become marshal of a tough trail town. He went from that to hunting down some border bandits.

Tex, his riders hired away or driven off, had sent the message south by the last rider who left him. Con Fargo had started north within the hour the message arrived. Yet he had reached Black Rock to learn that Tex Kilgore was dead.

It required no detailed study to understand what had happened. The Texan's enemies besieged him and he fought it out with them. Three had been killed and two wounded, and the attackers had had enough. They pulled out and abandoned the fight. What they didn't know was that one of the last bullets had left Kilgore dying on the cabin floor. A few days later they found out when a chuck line rider showed up with the news.

Only, Con Fargo, lean and frosty eyed, heard it at the same time. He noted the satisfaction on some faces, the indifference on others, and the harsh laughter of a few.

Putney, a huge mountain of a man, had turned to a lean Mexican.

"Mount up, Gomez!" he said. "We'll ride out and take over!"

"Sit still." Con, the stranger, lifted his voice just enough to bring stillness to the room. "I'm Kilgore's partner. I'm takin' over!"

"Another of 'em, huh?" Putney sneered. "You takin' over his fightin', too?"

"He was my friend," Con said simply. "If you were his enemy, you have two choices: get out of the country by sundown, or fill your hand!"

Putney was said to be a fast man. Black Rock changed its ratings on speed that day. Putney's six-gun never cleared leather. Con Fargo, one elbow on the bar, let Putney have the first one in the stomach, the second in the throat.

Gomez was a cunning man, but the sound of gunfire confused him. He went for his gun as the first shot sounded. He was against the wall on Fargo's right, while Putney was straight ahead of the former Ranger. Yet somehow the left hand, the elbow still on the bar, held a gun too. Fargo's head swung just for an instant, the second gun spouted fire, and Gomez hit the floor, clawing with both hands at the burning in his chest.

Con waited for a moment, letting his eyes survey the room. Then calmly holstering one gun, he thumbed cartridges into the other. He looked up then.

"My name's Con Fargo," he said pleasantly. "I'm goin' to be around here a long time. If," he continued, "any of you had a hand in killin' my pardner, you can join your friends on the floor, or start ridin'. Soon or late, I'll find out who you were."

He rode out to the Kilgore spread and took over. Twice, during the following week, he was shot at from ambush. The second sharpshooter failed to shoot sharp enough, or to move fast enough, having fired. Friends found him lying behind a rock with a bullet between his eyes.

Con Fargo rode alone. He had no friends, no intimates. In town they sold him what he needed, and once they tried to charge him twice what the supplies were worth. He paid the usual price, picked up his goods and left. Yet that very day he mailed a letter to some friends in Texas.

Then he found the dying man. Riding toward Massacre Rocks, he grinned wryly. After all, he had been a lawman, a badge toter. It was only natural that he try to find the killer of this man. Then, in a sense, it was his fight. Both had come into a country full of enemies.

Twice, after he reached the stage trail, Con slipped from the saddle to brush the snow from the road. Each time he found tracks of the buckboard, frozen solid. They headed right across the plain toward the black wall of Massacre Rocks.

Ambush was easy here. For twenty miles in any direction, there was only one way a man could get through the rock wall with a team: the gate at Massacre Rocks.

Fargo scouted it carefully and, finding no one, he rode on through. Here again he found wheel tracks. Then, fifty yards further, there were none. Backtracking, he noticed two strange circles under the thin snow. He walked over and kicked the snow from them. They were the iron tires from the buckboard. No doubt somewhere near would be the other two.

Soon he found a charred and partly burned wheel hub, and then he kicked the snow from a piece of what had been a seat. The cushion covered with an old, mostly burned wolf hide. Carrying the hub and the seat to the rocks he concealed them in a place where there was no snow to leave a mark.

It had been muddy and the murdered man had fallen. There should be marks in the red clay. Studying the situation, Con chose the most likely spot for the drygulcher to hide, and from that and the remnants of the burned buckboard, he found the end of the tracks.

Nearby, after sweeping several square yards of snow, he found where the wounded man had leaped from the buckboard, then the spot where he had gone to his knees. It was all there, frozen into the earth by the fierce norther.

And there, where the ambushed man had fallen, were boot tracks! Con Fargo knelt quickly. This was what he had been looking for. With his hunting knife he dug carefully around each track, then lifted the circles of frozen earth from the ground. He concealed them in another hollow in the rocks.

He mounted again and taking a cutoff through the mountains, rode into Sulphur Springs. From there he sent two messages, then strolled over to the livery stable. While he watered the mustang, he talked idly with the graybeard who worked around. "Got ary a buckboard for hire?" he asked.

"Yep! Only one, though. Young feller come in here few days ago and borrowed one. Hired her for a week. Pair of grays. Had some business over to Black Rock, I reckon. Somethin' about a ranch."

"Didn't say who he was, did he?"

"Nope. Wasn't very talkin'. Yank, by the sound of him. But he could handle them horses! Had him an old-time gun. One of them Patersons like the Rangers used years ago."

# Chapter 2
## *Saloon Brawl*

A raw, cold wind blew over the desert when he rode down off the mountains and skirted the wastelands, heading home. There was a light in his windows when he neared the cabin. Slipping from his horse, he crept across to the nearest window. What he saw inside brought a slow grin to his lips.

When his mustang was stabled he went up and pushed the door open.

"Howdy!" he said, grinning. "How's Texas?"

Two men sprang to their feet, then seeing his face, they began to grin.

"Con! By all that's holy! Glad to see you, boss!"

Bernie Quill, a slim youngster with a reckless face and blue eyes, shoved the plate of ham and eggs at Fargo.

"Set, and give us the lowdown. We come up here for a fight. Now don't tell us you've wound it all up!"

Briefly, he explained. José Morales rolled a cigarette and listened carefully.

"Then, señor," he said at last, "we do not know *who* we fight?"

"That's about it," Fargo agreed. "Tex cashed in before I got to him. Who killed him, I don't know. Putney and Gomez were probably in the gang, but they are dead. Still, I got some ideas.

"This place is in a notch of mountain, and Kilgore had control of twenty thousand acres of good grazing land north of the mountains. The Bar M and Lazy S control almost everything south of the mountains except the townsite of Black Rock.

"Tex come in here and found the pass that leads through the mountains from Black Rock. Those mountains look like a wall that a goat couldn't cross, but there's this one pass. So he moved in and took all the land north of the mountains over to the Springer Hills. The joke on the Lazy S and Bar M was that most of the rain falls north of the mountains.

"The Bar M is owned by an eastern syndicate, but all they ask is returns. The Lazy S is owned by Springer Bob Wakeman, old-timer, who made his and went back east to live. The Bar M is managed by Art Brenner, the Lazy S by Butch Mogelo."

*"Butch Mogelo?"* Quill's eyes narrowed. "Is he the hombre that killed Bill Priest down in Uvalde?"

"Same one," Fargo agreed. "Art Brenner is a big, handsome fellow, and from all I can figure out, a pretty smooth operator. I couldn't tie Putney or Gomez to either of them."

Yet the mention of Bob Wakeman's name started some pulse of memory throbbing. Something that wouldn't quite boil up into his consciousness was working in his mind. Springer Bob had been a friend of Fargo's back in the old trail-herding days. Once they had fought Comanches together down in the Nation. Con had been a boy of seventeen then, but doing a man's work. And had been for nearly four years.

Con got up when his supper was finished. "Morales, you come along with me." He glanced at Quill, grinning. "You stick around. And don't look so durned sour! You got as good a chance of having trouble as we do! I'm expectin' somebody to show up here. So keep your eyes open."

Two hours later Con Fargo walked up on the porch of the hotel and glanced around. The town was quiet enough. José Morales, per instructions, was tying his horse to the hitching rail down the street. They had come to town as strangers to each other.

Fargo stepped inside, just in time to hear laughter and then a polite, smooth voice.

"Yes, of course, Miss Wakeman," the voice said. "Tomorrow would be a good day to see the ranch—if it clears up a little. With all this snow, you know—" the words trailed off as he saw Con.

It was Art Brenner, but Con Fargo was not looking at him. He was looking past the tall foreman of the Bar M at the girl. And she was looking at him.

She was tall, with a graceful figure and a pretty mouth, a mouth losing its laughter now under his intent gaze. There was something hauntingly familiar in that face. Something he could not place—

Of course! It was the resemblance to her father!

"Howdy, Brenner," he said, ignoring the big man's coldness. "Did I hear you address the lady as Miss Wakeman?"

"That's right." Brenner's voice was crisp and sharp. "Now that you've learned that, you can move along. Miss Wakeman has no desire to meet killers and gunmen!"

"Oh, but I do!" she protested suddenly. "I want to meet everyone out here! And haven't you already said it was necessary to have gunmen working for you and for us?"

Brenner's face reddened and Con stifled a chuckle as he stepped forward.

"Since Mr. Brenner doesn't want to introduce me, Miss Wakeman," he said gently, his eyes smiling, "my name is Con Fargo."

Her eyes widened. "Why, of course! I remember. You're in the big picture Daddy had over his desk! The picture of one of his cattle drives. Your name was on it. But I'd never have recognized you now."

"I've changed some. Maybe it's getting older that matters." He could see the cool, quick appraisal in the girl's eyes, and something told him this girl was no fainting or helpless miss. She was, something told him, a daughter of her father.

"It will be nice having an old friend of Dad's near us," she said sincerely.

"Fargo's scarcely a friend," Brenner interrupted. His eyes were cold. "He's the one who settled on that land I told you we'd need. The land your father wanted so badly!"

"Oh, he is? But Mr. Brenner, I don't remember him ever saying anything about it!"

Brenner smiled easily. "Well, he probably didn't talk business with a young girl. He told us."

Con sensed instantly that Brenner had said the

wrong thing. Audrey Wakeman, he recalled her name now, was not the kind of a girl who liked being considered helpless.

"The land we settled on was considered inaccessible until we settled there," Fargo said quietly. "Your father would have had no trouble with us."

"You said 'we'?" Audrey said quickly. "Your wife?"

"My partner, Tex Kilgore. I'm not married." Then he said quietly, "Nor do I have a partner now. He was besieged in his cabin and murdered."

"Murdered?"

"Kilgore took land he had no right to!" Brenner protested sharply. "He was no better than an outlaw!"

"He took land as it has always been taken in the West," Fargo said bluntly. "Tex Kilgore has a record that will stand beside any man's. Beside yours, Brenner! He was an honest man and fought the cause of the law wherever it went."

Was it his imagination? Or had Brenner's face tightened when he made the reference to a record?

"Who killed him?" Audrey asked quickly.

"I don't know." Con Fargo shrugged. "Yet."

"Howdy, Brenner. Hello, Miss Wakeman!" The deep voice filled the room. Fargo turned, knowing what he would see, knowing that ever since he had come north he had known this moment would come.

Butch Mogelo, boss of the Lazy S, was not quite as tall as Con, but he was broad and thick. His square, brutal jaw rested solidly on a bull neck, his nose had been broken, and there was a scar over an eyebrow. He gave an impression of brutal power such as Fargo had never seen in any other man.

His small eyes fastened on Con Fargo, and instant recognition came to them. "So?" He stared at Brenner, then at Fargo again.

"You'll be Fargo, then? I never knowed your name."

"You two know each other?" Brenner's voice was sharp.

"Yeah," Mogelo snapped, "he used to be a Ranger. I knowed him in Texas."

"A *Ranger*?" This time there was no doubt. There was genuine shock in Brenner's voice. "Con Fargo—a Ranger?"

"So was Kilgore," Con said quietly. His eyes shifted from Brenner to Mogelo. Audrey Wakeman, he observed, was taking it all in, her eyes alert.

"The last time I saw you, Butch," he said, "you got out of Uvalde in time to keep from being asked some questions about a murder."

Mogelo's eyes were ugly. "You accusin' me?" he snarled. "I'll kill you, if you do!"

Fargo laughed carelessly. "When I accuse you of murder, Butch," he said sharply, "there won't be any doubt about what I'm saying!"

He turned on his heel, nodding to Audrey Wakeman, and walked from the room. Down the street was the Silver Bar. He pushed through the swinging doors and went in.

Morales was at the end of the bar with a drink in front of him. Nearer, four men were bellied against the bar, and all of them were Lazy S riders. Keller, Looby, Cabaniss, and Ross. He had taken care to know who rode for both big ranches, and something about them.

Keller was the troublemaker here. Cabaniss the most dangerous. All of the men were gunslingers.

Art Keller looked up as he stepped to the bar, and said something in a low tone to Mace Looby, who stood near him.

Morales lifted his glass and looked over it at Fargo and lifted an eyebrow. Morales was deadly with a six-gun, and with the knife he carried he was lightning itself.

Con wasn't thinking of the four Lazy S riders, he was thinking of Audrey Wakeman. What was she doing in Black Rock? Why had she come here? He knew how much money Springer Bob had lavished on his daughter, knew he had planned for her to marry eastern wealth. He knew she had had the best of educations and every advantage.

Obviously, she had come in on the stage that afternoon, for it was the first stage in several days. The thought of her going to the ranch with Mogelo chilled him. He knew the man. Butch Mogelo had been the suspect in a brutal murder of a husband, wife, and sister near Uvalde. There had been insufficient evidence to hold him, and he left the country ahead of the lynching party.

Art Keller edged closer to him along the bar.

"When you leavin' the country?" he demanded bluntly.

Con Fargo looked up. "I'm not leaving, Keller. Neither are you."

"You're blasted right I'm . . ." he broke off in midsentence, staring at Fargo. "What do you mean?" he demanded, puzzled.

"If you don't keep your hand away from that gun when you talk to me, you'll never leave this country. You'll be planted right here.

"And another thing," he continued before Keller could speak, "stay away from my range, do you hear? I've seen the tracks of that crowbait of yours, and if I catch you ridin' on my range, I'll set you afoot without your boots!"

Keller was stumped. He had started out to provoke a quarrel, and suddenly it was staring him in the face and he didn't like the look of it at all. Backed by three tough men, he had thought to run a blazer on Fargo. The play was suddenly taken away from him, and he suddenly realized that if shooting did start, he was going to be in an awfully hot spot.

Unable to see a way out, he started to bluster. "You'll do nothin'," he sneered. "Why, I'd—"

Con Fargo stepped close to him, and stared into Keller's eyes. Con's were suddenly icy, and Keller felt his mouth go dry.

"Why wait, Keller? Why not try it now?"

Keller took a step back, wetting his lips.

"Go ahead, Keller," Ross said. "Give him a whippin'!"

Others were staring at him. A dozen of the townspeople were in the saloon, and Chance, the saloon owner, was leaning over the bar, watching.

Keller swung. What happened to the punch he never knew. Hard knuckles drove into his teeth, and something struck him a wicked blow in the wind, then an iron-hard fist smashed him on the angle of the jaw, and he folded into darkness.

It had happened so suddenly that Cabaniss and the others were caught flat-footed. They had expected trouble, had been ready for it. They had waited here hoping to get Fargo in a killing spot. Now they had him, but so suddenly they were unprepared.

Con Fargo, his feet spread, hands held high, was staring at Cabaniss.

"All right, Steve," Con said quietly. "This is it. If you want to buy chips, here's your chance."

Mace Looby moved out from Steve, his eyes watchful. Ross moved away from Looby. The three men spread fanwise, faced him. Con smiled without otherwise changing expression.

"Which one do you want, José?" he said. "You can only have one."

Steve Cabaniss, his hands poised, suddenly froze. Consternation swept over his face, and Mace Looby, almost on tiptoes, settled back on his heels.

"Give to me this Steve, if you please," Morales said smoothly. "I like to shoot him full of holes."

Lucky Chance, the saloon owner, was smiling coldly and with appreciation. He started to speak, but before the words could leave his mouth, Con Fargo moved. His movement was so sudden, and came so closely on the heels of their shocked surprise, that the three men were again caught unprepared.

Con took one leap forward and smashed Looby over the head with the barrel of his six-gun. Looby crashed to the floor, and Fargo lashed left and right. Ross went down as if struck by lightning, and Cabaniss, struck a glancing blow, tottered back against the bar, blood streaming into his eyes.

Fargo was on him even as Steve's hand dropped for a gun. Slapping the hand away, Con hooked a short right to the chin, and Cabaniss hit the floor in a heap.

"Nice work, Fargo," Chance said quietly. "I've been hoping to see that happen for a long time."

Con Fargo grinned at him, then turned to go. Butch Mogelo was standing just inside the door.

Astonishment blanked his face, then fury.

"What's goin' on here?" he snarled.

"Your boys got a little troublesome," Con said evenly. "I almost thought they were tryin' to trap me into a three-cornered fight and button me up."

"You slugged my boys?" Mogelo's face was dark with fury. "Why!" Suddenly, he straightened a little, and the fury left his face. "Huh," he said gruffly, "maybe they was askin' for it."

Striding past Fargo he grabbed Ross and jerked him to his feet. Then Looby and Cabaniss. Staggering, the three stumbled out the door ahead of him.

"Well, I'll be hanged!" Chance said. "You bluffed him!"

"No," Fargo replied slowly, "I didn't." Thoughtfully, he stared after Mogelo. What had made the man change so suddenly? Butch Mogelo was not yellow. Brute that he might be, he had the courage of his brutality. There was something more behind this.

José Morales moved up beside Con as the tall gunfighter stepped out the door.

"Something is wrong, no?" Morales suggested.

Fargo nodded. "Mogelo and Brenner are thick as thieves. They got something planned."

He scowled as they took the trail back to the ranch. Who was the stranger who had been murdered? What was Audrey Wakeman doing in Black Rock? How did it happen that Brenner and Mogelo were so close?

Somehow, some way, he must talk to Audrey. He had a hunch that a talk with her might prove the solution to the puzzle. He was no longer so sure that it was jealousy or range rivalry that had brought about the death of Tex Kilgore. There was something deeper, something stirring beneath the obvious, beneath the surface showings.

What, after all, did he know? Tex Kilgore had been killed, apparently by a number of men who had besieged the cabin. Yet they were obviously acting at someone's command. And was it only because he held a desirable bit of range?

Who was the stranger? Why had he not come into Black Rock on the stage? Why had he left the stage at Sulphur Springs and hired a buckboard to drive in? Who had killed him?

Fargo had the murdered man's clothing with what evidence it offered. He had concealed the charred hub, the partly burned cushion, the frozen tracks. Yet, aside from the tracks, which might or might not prove anything, he had only evidence to show the man was murdered, the buckboard destroyed, and all evidence of identity wiped out. He had nothing that pointed to the killer.

Butch Mogelo was a killer, but Butch was not the man to rip the labels from a man's clothing and destroy evidence so carefully. Mogelo had been an outlaw and a rustler. How did that tie in here?

## Chapter 3
### Jailbreak

The following night, after the two hands had headed off
for town, Con opened the hole in the floor and got out
the clothes once more. Carefully, he went over them,
but they offered no new clue. He stowed them away, as
puzzled as ever.

When Bernie Quill and Morales rode in, he met
them at the door. "Some news," Quill said. "There's a
U.S. marshal in town and a Pinkerton detective. Art
Brenner was eatin' dinner with 'em."

Early the next morning Con Fargo mounted up
and headed for town. When he was still several miles
out, he saw Audrey Wakeman riding toward him from
down a hillside. He reined in, waiting.

"Howdy!" he said cheerfully.

She nodded, but her manner was cool.

"Miss Wakeman," he asked, "I wonder if you'd
mind tellin' me why you came west?"

Audrey glanced at him, surprise and some suspicion in her eyes.

"Why do you ask?" she demanded.

"Maybe it might help to straighten out some diffi-
culties," he said.

"All right," she said crisply, "I'll tell you: I came
because we've been losing cattle. Ever since my father
died the income from the ranch has been falling off, and
Mr. Mogelo tells me our cattle are being rustled."

Fargo nodded. "I figured maybe it was somethin'
like that. Did he have any ideas who was rustlin' them?"

She hesitated, then her eyes flashed. "He said the
rustling started when Tex Kilgore moved in here. It
hasn't let up any since you came!"

Con's eyes hardened. "Did he tell you he had
made rustlin' a profession in Texas? That he did time in
prison for it?"

"I trust my foreman, Mr. Fargo." Her manner was

crisp. "You, having ridden with my father, should be a friend of his, and of mine."

"What makes you think I'm not?" he asked gently. "There's two sides to every story."

Her chin lifted stubbornly, and she kept her eyes looking ahead. "All right, what's yours?"

He shrugged. "That I never rustled a cow in my life, ma'am. That no more honest man ever lived than Tex Kilgore. That he knew your pappy afore I did, and worked for him for years. That somehow you got a thief and an outlaw for a foreman, and personally, I don't think Brenner's any better."

Her face flushed. "You've evidence to back that, I expect?"

"No," he said frankly, "I haven't."

"Then you'd better keep your accusations to yourself! I don't think Mr. Brenner would like them!" She touched spurs to her horse.

He watched the cloud of dust and stared ruefully after her.

"Well," he muttered, "you sure didn't do yourself no good that time!"

Art Brenner was a smooth-talking man, and he had a way with women. It was making itself felt. Obviously, whatever doubts she may have had were lulled to sleep now. Art Brenner and Butch Mogelo were riding high.

Yet, he did know something. He knew that he had rustled no stock. He knew that Tex Kilgore was a man who would never have dreamed of rustling stock. He knew that Butch Mogelo had been a rustler by profession. Therefore, the chances were that Butch had rustled the stock himself.

But where had it gone?

The town was quiet when he rode in. He dismounted and walked into the saloon. Chance was standing at the end of the bar, and he nodded. Then as Con ordered a drink, he glanced up.

"Better watch, friend. They are brewing big medicine. I think it's for you."

"Could be." He glanced obliquely at Chance. "Know anything about Brenner?"

Chance's lips tightened. "No. And I'm not a talkin' man." He took a swallow of whiskey. "However, he was ridin' a big horse when he came into town. And it had done some fast travelin'.'"

He walked away and went into his office. Fargo scowled over the idea. A big horse? What did he mean by that? Then a thought struck him. In the north, where there was lots of snow, they used bigger horses than in the south. This wasn't really snow country. The present storm was unusual, and probably the snow wouldn't last long.

So? Art Brenner came from the north, and he was traveling fast. He looked up to see Bernie Quill.

The boyish cowhand lined up beside him at the bar.

"Boss, better light out. I hear they got a warrant for you. For murder!"

"Bernie," Fargo said quietly. "Get over to Sulphur Springs and see if there's any messages for me. Also, send messages to these five towns." Quickly he noted down the message to send and the towns. "Then you and José take turns hunting the hills, I think our place is the best bet, for some rustled cattle."

Quill turned, and just then the door opened. Art Brenner stood there, and beside him were two strange men. Behind them were Mace Looby, his face dark and ugly, and the thin, saturnine face of Steve Cabaniss.

"I'm Spilman," the first man said. He was lean, elderly, cold eyed. "Deputy United States marshal for this territory. You're under arrest for murder."

"Murder?" he asked. "Who am I supposed to have killed?" Suddenly, he saw Mogelo come in, and beside him was Audrey Wakeman. Her face was pale and tight with scorn.

"Billy Wakeman," Spilman said coldly. "Bob Wakeman's son!"

"That's nonsense!" he said. "I never killed him. I never saw the hombre."

"Esslinger," Spilman said, jerking his thumb at the detective. "Tell him!"

"We found his body buried in an abandoned drift on your place, and we found his clothes hidden under your floor!"

Con Fargo felt dry and empty inside. He'd never thought of that. They had him clinched.

"I didn't kill him!" he protested. "I'd no idea who he was!"

"You didn't know?" Esslinger asked skeptically. "You deny burying him?"

"No," he said, "I buried him. I found him in the snow. He'd been drygulched by someone. I took him home and worked over him all durin' the storm. He died without recoverin' consciousness."

Brenner laughed coldly. "Likely story! What did you hide his clothes for? Why didn't you report him being dead?"

"Because I wanted to find the killer," Con said slowly, knowing they wouldn't believe. "I figured," he studied Brenner as he spoke, "he was a man with something to hide. Somethin' more than stolen cattle."

Audrey kept her face averted as he was led from the room. He saw Bernie Quill mounting his horse, and then they took him away to jail. They started to turn away then.

"Wait a minute," he said. Spilman and Esslinger turned.

"Marshal, I wish you'd get in touch with Ransom, in El Paso," he said. "Ask him about Tex Kilgore, and about me."

"The Ranger captain?" Spilman studied him coldly. "Why?"

"Both of us were Rangers. There's something more here than meets the eye, Spilman. Why didn't Wakeman come right to Black Rock, instead of getting off the stage at Sulphur Springs? Ask yourself that. Then tell me who tipped you off that I had the clothes?"

"Mogelo. He went to your cabin, glanced in the window and saw you hidin' them. Then we hunted for the body today while you were gone." Esslinger studied him. "Why do you think Wakeman got off at the Springs?" Then he added, "And how do you know he did?"

"I think it was because he didn't want his own ranch foreman to know he was comin'. I think he wanted a little private look around. I know he got off there because he hired a rig in the Springs. He was drygulched at Massacre Rocks, the rig burned, the horses taken away."

Esslinger looked at Spilman. "Well, he's tellin' us how it was done."

Fargo kept his eyes on Spilman. "Something else you might think over. The hombre at the livery stable told me the kid had a Paterson thirty-four caliber. It wasn't on his body. Maybe the killer threw it away. And then again, maybe he kept it."

Carefully, he explained the finding of the body, the final shot. "Figure it for yourselves," he said. "Why, if I had the clothes, would I tear out the labels? Wouldn't I have burned them? Anyway you look at it, just tearing the labels out doesn't make sense. The man who killed Billy Wakeman expected the body to be found when the snow went off—without any identification."

Con slid a hand in his shirt pocket and brought out the notes he had taken from the dead man.

"See? I took these because I figured to find out who was killed, and why."

Spilman cleared his throat. "You make it sound good," he said, and turned on his heel. Esslinger followed him out.

Fargo gripped the bars, staring after them. His words seemed to have had no effect. Knowing the summary way of most western courts, and how all newcomers were disliked here, he realized he had small chance. Most of all, he was hurt by Audrey Wakeman's willingness to believe him guilty. Art Brenner had done his work well.

He had an idea what was behind it all, but without proof his idea amounted to nothing.

No matter how much he believed Brenner to be the motivating force behind the trouble and the killings, without proof it meant nothing. The fact that Mogelo had been an outlaw and killer also meant nothing, for many men in the west had outlived tough reputations to become respected citizens.

Much would depend on what Quill and Morales could find. And such a search might require months, for the hills east and west of his own place were probably unknown to anyone.

For two days he paced the floor, growing more and more anxious. Spilman came in occasionally, bringing his food. He saw no one else. Then José came in, followed by Spilman. The marshal watched them a moment and then went back inside the office.

"This Esslinger? He go up the hills. I see him. Two day he no come back. Bernie Quill he go, he no come back."

Fargo scowled. Now what? If Esslinger had gone into the mountains, it could mean the Pinkerton man had believed him. But still, why to the hills? He had not even suggested his own theory to the man. He shook his head.

"José," he said, "get me two blocks of wood about six inches long, two inches thick. Bring them back here. Then go back to the ranch and keep a sharp eye out."

"Two blocks of wood?" José shrugged, his eyes puzzled. "It makes no sense." He turned and went out.

Con Fargo yelled for the marshal, and when the lean old man came up to the bars, he grinned at him.

"Listen," he said, "I'm goin' nuts. How about something to do? How about a file, or a saw."

"Nothin' doin'!" Spilman said. He spat. "You're not gettin' out of this calaboose, son, I promise you!"

"Well, I can whittle, can't I? At least let me have a couple of sticks and a knife."

Spilman shrugged. "All right, all right! I'll tell that Mex cowhand of yourn."

A few minutes later, the door opened and José, with Spilman at his elbow, brought in the blocks of wood.

"This marshal say bring sticks," José said, smiling.

Twice, later in the evening, Spilman walked to the bars. Con was busy, carving a wooden horse. He grinned at Spilman.

"Marshal," he said, "when I get this horse finished I'm goin' to ride him right out of here!"

Spilman grinned, his frosty eyes softening a little.

"If you can ride out of here on a wooden horse, you can go!" he said cheerfully. "Not a bad horse, at that!" he added, grudgingly.

When the marshal had gone, Fargo slipped the other block of wood from under the blanket and went to work. Three hours later, an hour after Spilman went out, closing the office door after him, Con was ready.

"Now, let's pray that lock is well oiled!" he said.

In his hand he held a six-inch wooden key, neatly carved from the second block of wood.

"Lucky you noticed that key when he opened the door for chow," he said to himself. "Now if this'll only work!"

Carefully he inserted the key in the massive lock. Slowly he turned it. As naturally as though it was the original key, the lock turned and the door opened. Softly, he closed it after him.

Grinning, Fargo picked up the wooden horse and stepped out into the office. His guns hung from a nail on the wall. Belting them on, he shouldered into the buffalo coat, feeling the other gun as he did so. Pocketing the wooden key, he placed the wooden horse in the middle of the marshal's desk. Then picking up his rifle, he slid out through a crack of the door.

It was snowing again. He crept around the wall of the jail and started for the trees. Yet he had scarcely reached them when he heard a low voice.

"Here, señor!"

"José!" he said. "You here?"

"With two horses, señor boss. José he think, mebbe so this boss have one idea, no? Perhaps she work."

Mounting, they turned up through the timber, skirted around and headed for the hills. As they rode, Morales talked. Bernie Quill was still missing on his search into the hills. Nor had Esslinger returned. Did he know the way taken by Quill?

"*Sí, señor.* Each day we mark on map how we go, how much we search. Bit by bit we cross off the map. Now is left only a little bit."

The snow was falling fast, but winds had blown earlier snow from the trail, or what remained had become hard packed. They made fast time. Con Fargo was laboring under no delusion. Spilman would be after them. When he returned to the jail, he would look in on his prisoner before turning in, and when he found him gone he would not wait for daybreak. Yet, if Fargo could get into the hills, there was a chance he could trail Bernie Quill. He could not believe the young puncher was dead.

It would be deathly cold in the mountains, no weather for any man to be out at night. Esslinger, too, was gone.

They rounded the last turn of the trail, and Morales grasped his arm.

"Señor, a light!"

The cabin windows were aglow. Bernie, perhaps? He slid from the saddle at the door.

"José, saddle two fresh horses—the buckskin and the grulla!" He swung the door open and stepped inside.

Audrey Wakeman stood, her face white, in the center of the floor.

"You? . . . *Here*?" He walked toward her, shedding the buffalo coat and dropping it on the bed.

"Yes." She stepped toward him. "How can you ever forgive me? I thought you'd killed my brother, and then I found this." She held out the Paterson .34, her brother's gun.

"Where'd you find it?" he demanded.

The voice that cut across his words was sharp and even.

"Hold right still, Fargo! And don't get any ideas, if you haven't guessed, I'm Bent Ryler!"

"Sure," Con said, "I guessed, Brenner! You were too durned scary about Rangers. Then I got a tip you'd come from the north. That made me guess who you was. Bent Ryler was wanted for murder in Butte."

Ryler sneered. "Doesn't do you much good, does it? The great Con Fargo, under my guns!" He smiled quizzically. "Might have been quite a show at that, Fargo. Ryler and Fargo! They say we're two of the fastest men in the west."

"Do they?" Con shrugged. "Ryler, you're a tinhorn and you know it. You never saw the day you could draw with me. You got the drop, so you can talk, but with an even break . . . man, you wouldn't have a chance."

"No?" Bent Ryler's face hardened. "Well, if it's an even break you're fishing for, you won't get it. Nobody knows I'm Bent Ryler but you and the girl here. They still call me Brenner. In a few minutes I'm going to drop you, and then when I'm through with her, she won't want to talk."

The door opened and Keller came in with Ross. They grinned at Fargo and covered him with their guns.

Keller's mean little eyes gleamed with triumph. "Got you, huh?" he said.

That Ryler would kill him, Fargo had no doubt. The man was cold-blooded and had always been. If only Audrey were not here! Without her, he could take a chance. Still, death might be a break for her. Bent Ryler was no break for any girl.

Where was José? Had they got him?

"I'm going to kill you, Fargo," Ryler said. He slipped his guns back into their holsters. His lips thinned. The fingers on his hands spread, hovering over his guns. "When I do, I'm goin' to let you see what a fast draw is!"

Suddenly, there was a crash of broken glass, and José's smooth voice said:

"If you please to lift the hands?" The rifle barrel was wavering between Keller and Ross.

Ryler swore, and his hands dropped. Fargo glimpsed their blurring speed; then a gun thundered and Ryler, his gun clear of the holster, stopped with his hand half lifted. He teetered on his feet, an expression of blank astonishment on his face.

Almost unconsciously, Con Fargo had drawn and fired. Now, he fired again. Bent Ryler's gun boomed at the floor, and then he crumpled to the boards.

"You beat me!" he gasped, amazement frozen into his features.

Con Fargo faced the others. Keller was back against the wall, blood dripping from his right hand. Ross was down on the floor. Con had never even heard the shots that stopped them.

# Chapter 4
## Bullets for Payment

Quickly the door swung open and Morales came in. Behind him were Marshal Spilman and Lucky Chance with three other men, all armed.

Spilman glanced at the men on the floor, then at Fargo.

"What happened here?" he demanded sternly.

Quickly, Fargo explained. When he had finished, Audrey Wakeman nodded.

"What he said is true, Mr. Spilman. I reached here just a few minutes before Brenner—Ryler, I mean.

"He was riding to the Bar M with me, and we stopped in passing his place. I waited in the house while he gave some orders, and saw a heavy coat hanging on a hook. The butt of a gun was visible from the pocket, so I took it out—I guess there was something familiar about it. Then I saw it was Billy's Paterson. I knew it from a scratch on the butt.

"I ran outside and got on my horse and rode here as quickly as I could. I wanted help, and then I was," she hesitated, glancing at Con, "awfully sorry for accusing him when I had known Mr. Fargo was my father's friend."

Spilman stared at the bodies thoughtfully; then he looked up at Fargo.

"I never was sure," he said. "Your story sounded good. Esslinger, he figured you was guilty. But then he says to me that while he's sure, he's goin' to check up. I ain't seen him since."

A faint yell sounded from outside, and Fargo lunged to the door. They scrambled out of the way, and he threw the door open. A weary horse was struggling through the snow. One man was on his back, another over the saddle in front of him. The rider was Bernie Quill.

"Hurry!" he said faintly. "I guess I'm—all in!"

Morales grabbed him as he fell. The second man was Esslinger. The detective had been shot twice. Quill had a hole in his leg and one trouser leg was soaked with blood.

One of the possemen swung into the saddle and started for town and a doctor. Fargo went swiftly to work on Esslinger while Audrey Wakeman cut away Quill's trouser leg and began to bathe the leg wound.

Quill's eyes fluttered open. "Never reckoned you'd be workin' on no wound for me, ma'am," he said, grinning faintly. He looked up at Spilman. "Esslinger found the rustled cattle, same time I did. Then Cabaniss and Looby rode up on him. They shot him down. Me, I was under cover, so I opened up and drove 'em off.

"I got Esslinger into the woods, and we holed up in a cave. He was in durned bad shape, and they kept me so busy I couldn't help much. He's game, though, plenty game! He told me what happened."

Bernie's face twisted with pain. "He got busy after Con talked to him at the jail. Didn't figure it was true, but he checked at Sulphur Springs, then checked Massacre Rocks. Then he found out about the messages Con sent, askin' about recent shipments of cattle. That gave him a lead, and he puts it all together, like Con done, and figured there must be rustled cows in the mountains."

Spilman looked around as Con got up. "Lost blood, mostly. The doc can tell you more'n I can. I reckon he may get through, all right. Somebody'd better find a way to get more blood into a wounded man, shot like that."

"What happened, Fargo?" Spilman asked. "What was goin' on?"

"The way I figure it, Mogelo and Ryler worked out a deal between 'em. Kilgore figured he was the first to find that pass, but Mogelo and Ryler were usin' that pass to get rustled cattle out. They had a place back there somewheres, where they was holdin' cattle, then shippin' 'em out.

"When Tex moved in, he camped right across their trail. They couldn't get in to the cattle without being seen, and they couldn't smuggle no more through the pass. By accident he sure choused up the layout for 'em.

"If they was goin' on with the rustlin' and they maybe figured to bust up both ranches and buy 'em cheap—they had to get Kilgore out of there."

Quill's eyes opened again. "Indian Valley," he said. "They got about six hundred head of cows and two mighty fine gray horses up in that valley."

"Two gray horses?" Fargo turned to the marshal. "There it is, Spilman. Those were the horses Wakeman hired from the livery stable at the Springs. I've got the footprints of the killer stuck in a hole in the rocks down there, and a piece of the wheel hub, too."

Spilman turned. "Well, Chance, you and the boys come along and we'll pick up Butch Mogelo and his pals!"

When they had gone, Audrey walked over to Con. She put her hand on his sleeve.

"I'm sorry, Con. I don't think I ever really believed it, but when they found Billy's body here and his clothes. . . . Well, it was so much evidence, and then, Ryler was so smooth about it. He made it seem obvious that you should be the one."

She looked up at Con. "Daddy always liked you, Con. You were his favorite. Time and again he used to wonder what ever became of you. He used to say he hoped Billy would be half the man you were."

Quill opened his eyes. "Didn't Daddy say nothin' 'bout me? Shucks, now. That ain't fair!"

"Shut up!" Fargo said, grinning. "You're a wounded man!"

Horses' hoofs beat on the hardpacked snow. Glancing around, Con's face went pale.

"Audrey," he said quickly. "Stay out of sight! It's Butch Mogelo."

Quickly, he checked his guns, then stepped to the door. He opened it and stepped out on the snow.

It was a gray day; flat, expressionless clouds lay across the sky, and a chill wind whispered through the pines. Butch Mogelo had dropped from the saddle. Steve Cabaniss and Mace Looby still sat their horses.

"Looks like the showdown," Butch said, grinning through his broken teeth. "You busted up a good deal, Fargo. Now we bust one up for you!

"Waited back there," he jerked his head at the trees, "until the marshal rode off. Reckoned to have you here alone. Then, when we get through with you, we can finish off that detective and that kid cowhand of yourn."

"Con," Quill's voice sounded from the door. "If you'll shift a little when the shootin' starts I'll be durned pleased to show Mogelo this kid cowhand can handle a six-gun."

Propped against the doorjamb, Bernie Quill stared at the three, smiling pleasantly.

Snow crunched at the stable door, and Con's quick eye caught the lazy figure of José Morales. "Sí, señor," he said. "You have send for Quill and I for the fight. Now here it is!"

Butch Mogelo's face twisted. "Evened it up, huh? Well, let it go this way, then." His big hands swept down.

Con stepped aside and started blasting with his right-hand gun. His first bullet turned Mogelo half around, and then the big man steadied down and opened up. The bullet knocked Con's hat into the snow, and Fargo fired his gun twice more, holding it low.

He could hear the pounding of other guns, saw Cabaniss topple into the snow, struggle to get up, and then be smashed back as though struck by a mighty fist. He walked toward Mogelo, snapping another shot. The big man's face was twisted with hate.

The big gun in his hand came up, and he was sneering. He went to his knees, then got up. Chill wind blew across Con's face, drying the sweat. He spread his legs and using the border shift, swapped hands with his guns. He turned his left side away, and fired fast, two quick shots. Mogelo's face was struck blank, and then across the sudden whiteness came a thin trickle of blood. He took one slow, questioning step forward, and fell on his face.

The sudden stillness after the sound of guns was like death. Con, unhurt, glanced across at José Morales. The Mexican was leaning against the doorjamb of the stable.

"One small scratch!" he said. "It is good shooting, no?"

"Quill?" Fargo turned.

"All right," Bernie said. "Threw splinters in my face a couple of times. Those boys weren't smart. They should have hit the snow sooner."

Con walked over to Butch Mogelo. The big outlaw was dead. Three shots had gone through his body, one through the muscles where his neck joined his shoulder, and the last one between the eyes.

Cabaniss had been hit three times. At least two of the wounds, one inflicted by Morales and one by Quill, would have been fatal.

Mace Looby was still alive, sitting in the snow.

He looked up at Fargo.

"My luck run out," he said, and died.

Morales walked toward the house, wiping blood from his cheekbone.

"You inherit much trouble, *sí*?"

Con Fargo turned and looked up at the pines clothing the long razor-backed ridge.

"Yeah," he said. "A lot of trouble, but a wonderful country—a man's country!"

"No room for a woman?" Audrey said from the door.

He looked at her, smiling slowly. "A western woman," he said.

Audrey said quickly, "My mother rocked me to sleep in a prairie schooner with a rifle across her knees."

"That's western!" Fargo said, and slipping an arm around her waist they walked through the door together.

# AUTHOR'S NOTE
# RIDING

*Rodeos have produced some great riders, and I've been fortunate enough to know some of the very best, but the most fun riding I ever saw—and some of the best— was down on the Big Sandy in Arizona when some of the local boys were getting in shape to try rodeo riding.*

*They rounded up some rough stock from the wild country, horses that had never been ridden by anybody, and they tried their luck. There was nobody around to blow a whistle and nobody to pick them off when their time was up. They got into the saddle and, if they could, rode the horse to a finish—and some of those horses seemed to have read the book and gone to school when it came to bucking.*

*Those kids, most of them fifteen to twenty-five, had been riding all their lives, getting into the saddle on frosty mornings when a horse figures it's his right to put his rider into the nearest prickly pear patch or whatever is available.*

*It wasn't my kind of riding. I always preferred placid, contemplative horses that had nowhere in particular they wanted to go.*

*When those boys rode, it was for their own pleasure, and there was no audience except some more of their own kind or a few older cowboys who had graduated from that sort of thing years before and now were perfectly willing to watch.*

*There were a couple of brothers among the older cowboys, however, who had made a name for themselves in rodeo areas. They had a brother named John who, if he would ride, was the best of them all.*

*There was a hammer-headed roan with a mean eye (I patterned Chick Bowdrie's horse after him) who just seemed to smile when a cowboy put a boot in his stirrup. Whatever there was to know about bucking, that roan knew, but it was what he invented on the spur of the moment that played Hob with the boys.*

*He'd piled several of them without working up a good lather, and they all egged John into trying him, until finally he gave in.*

*It was a ride that would have taken first money at Cheyenne or Calgary, but instead it happened on a frosty morning in Arizona with only fifteen or twenty people standing around to watch.*

*John rode him all right, rode him a good two or three minutes and then unloaded and ducked through the poles of the corral with that roan right after him, teeth bared.*

*Soon after, I left that part of the country, but I'll not forget what John said when they asked if he'd ride that roan again. It wasn't very original and it wasn't witty, but it was explicit. He simply said, "Not for all the money in the world!"*

*It was the way he said it that mattered. I don't know what happened to John or the roan, but I've never forgotten that ride.*

# Rowdy Rides to Glory

## Chapter 1
### *For Want of a Horse*

Rowdy Horn stared gloomily at Cub's right hind leg and shook his head with regret.

"No use even thinkin' about it, Jenny," he admitted ruefully to the girl he wanted to marry. "Cub won't work at the Stockman's Show this year. Not with that leg!"

Jenny Welman nodded, faintly irritated. Something was always going wrong. "No," she agreed, "you can't ride him, and without a good roping horse you wouldn't have a chance at first money, and without five thousand dollars—"

"I know! Without it we can't get married!" Rowdy ran his fingers through his dark, curly hair. "Jenny, does that money make so much difference? Lots of folks I know started with a darned sight less, and if I get a good calf crop this year we would be all set."

"We've talked of this before," Jenny replied quietly. "If you want to marry me, you've got to provide a home for me. I won't start like my mother did."

"She was pretty happy," Horn insisted stubbornly, "and your mother was a mighty fine woman."

"True, but just the same, I want to be comfortable! I don't want to slave my youth away trying to get ahead like she did." Suddenly, and excitedly, Jenny caught his arm. "Rowdy! I just happened to think. Why don't you see Bart Luby?"

"Luby?" Horn's mouth tightened. "What would I see him for?"

"Maybe he would let you borrow Tanglefoot to ride! He's going to ride Royboy, I know, so why don't you ride over and ask him?"

"Ask a favor of Bart Luby?" Rowdy's eyes smoldered. "I will not! I'll let the rodeo go to kingdom come, and the ranch too, before I'll go to him for help! Anyway, he'd turn me down flat. He knows well enough that with Cub and me out of the running he is a cinch to win."

"Will it do any harm to ask?" Jenny insisted impatiently. "Why you imagine he holds anything against you, I can't guess. He's the wealthiest man in the whole South Rim country, and has the biggest ranch, so why he should worry about you, I wouldn't know."

There was an undercurrent in Jenny's voice that stirred Rowdy's resentment. He glanced up, studying her carefully. He had been in love with Jenny Welman for a long time, and had been going around with her for almost a year, yet somehow of late he had been experiencing vague doubts. Nothing he could put his finger on, but little things led him to believe that she placed more emphasis upon whether a man had money than how he got it.

"If you'd like," she suggested, her eyes brightening, "I could see him for you."

"No." Horn shook his head stubbornly. "I won't ask him, and I don't want you asking him. He knows exactly how I feel about him, and he knows I think there was something wrong about that Bar O deal."

"But Rowdy!" she protested, almost angry. "How can you be so foolish? After three years I was hoping you'd forgotten that silly resentment you had because you didn't get that ranch."

"Well, I haven't!" Rowdy told her firmly. "If there was one man I knew, it was old Tom Slater, and I know what he thought of Bart. There was a time when he thought of leaving that ranch to both of us together, but after Bart Luby left and went to cattle buying, Slater never felt the same about him. Something happened then that old Tom didn't like. Why, three times he told me he didn't even want Luby on the place, and that he was leaving it to me. It doesn't make sense that he would change his mind at the last minute!"

"It was not at the last minute!" Jenny protested. "He had given Bart a deed to the ranch—over a year before his death. Why, with that deed he didn't even need the will, but all the same, the will left everything to him. You heard it read yourself."

Jenny's chin lifted, and in her eyes Rowdy Horn could see the storm signals flying. This old argument always irritated Jenny. She was just like nearly everybody in the South Rim: admired Luby's cash and show as well as his business ability. And of course, the man *had* made money.

It was easy to admire Bart Luby if you accepted him from the surface appearance. He had a dashing way, and he was a powerful man physically, handsome and smooth talking. He was the one who had the Stockman's Show organized, and for three years now had been featured in it for his fine riding, roping, and bulldogging. He was the local champion, because for those three years he had won all the major events.

But that will—that was something else.

Rowdy Horn was usually reasonable, but on the subject of that will he ceased being reasonable. It was flatly contradictory to everything he knew of Tom Slater, who had been almost a father to him.

Besides that, nobody could work with a man as Rowdy had worked with Bart Luby without knowing something of him, and Bart had always been unscrupulous in little things. He had left the Bar O to become a rodeo contest rider and a cattle buyer, and there had been vague rumors, never substantiated and never investigated, that his success as a buyer was due to his association—suspected only—with Jack Rollick.

Rollick was a known rustler who haunted the broken canyon country beyond the Rim, and did his rustling carefully and with skill among the brakes south of the Rim. It was hard to get proof of his depredations—nobody had, as yet—for he never drove off large numbers of cattle and never rustled any stock with unusual markings. He weeded cattle from the herds, or the lone steers that haunted the thick brush, and it was generally believed he gathered them in some interior valley to hold until he had enough to drive to market. Such shortages as his rustling caused would not show up until the roundup.

"Well, I'm riding back into Aragon, then, if you won't listen to a thing I say," Jenny said, swinging into her saddle. "But I do wish you'd change your mind and let me see Bart for you."

Rowdy shook his head, grinning up at her. Looking at him, Jenny thought for the thousandth time that he was easily the handsomest cowboy, the best-looking man afoot or in the saddle in the whole South Rim country. It was too bad he was so stubborn and such a poor manager.

"Don't worry," he said, smiling. "One way or another I'll be in that rodeo, and I'll win first money. Then we can be married."

She gave him her hand. "I know you will, dear. Luck."

With a wave of her hand, she wheeled the paint

and rode off at a snappy trot. He watched her go, uncertain again. Cub nickered plaintively, as if unaware of the disaster his misfortune had brought upon them.

Rowdy ran his hand under Cub's mane and scratched the horse's neck.

"Too bad, old boy. We worked mighty hard, trainin' you for that rodeo, and all for nothing. That hole you stepped into was sure in the wrong place."

Gravely, he studied the situation, but could see no way out, no escape. His Slash Bar was a small ranch, the place upon which Tom Slater had made his start. Rowdy had bought the ranch from the bank, making the down payment with his savings and the reward for the capture of Beenk Danek, a bank robber.

There had been a few good months after the ranch was his, then the roundup—and he had been missing more than two hundred head of cattle, more than any other one rancher, even those with much larger herds. His was small.

Then there had been fence trouble with Luby's men, although never with Luby himself, and more than once it had almost led to shooting. Despite Luby's smooth excuses, he was sure the cattleman was deliberately instigating trouble. To top it all, water shortages had developed, and he had fallen behind in his payments to the bank. So it had been the Stockman's Show and Rodeo that had offered him the best chance to make a substantial payment on the ranch as well as to provide the things on which Jenny insisted. Until Cub's injury, he had been certain he had at least an even chance with Bart Luby, and Bart had been aware of it, too.

Now still another worry had developed. One of his two hands, Mike McNulty, had ridden in a couple of days before to tell him the water hole at Point of Rocks was shrinking—the only water supply for miles of range. It had been considered inexhaustible. That was a matter which Rowdy must look into himself—and now.

Mounting a steeldust he used for rough riding, he started off for the dim and lonely land under the gigantic wall of the Rim. There, at the end of a trailing point of rocks, lay the water hole.

It was an hour's ride from the home ranch, and when he drew rein near the water hole the sun was still almost an hour high. His fears were realized the instant his eyes fell upon what always had been a wide, clear pool, for around it lay a rim, at least six feet wide, of gray mud, indicating the shrinkage. This was the last straw.

A hoof struck stone, and surprised, he glanced up. Lonely as this place was, other riders than the two men who worked for him hardly ever came to this water hole. But here was one—and a girl.

She was tall, slender, yet beautifully built. He wondered instantly who she was. He had never seen her before. Her dark hair was drawn to a loose knot at the nape of her neck, and her eyes were big and dark. She was riding a splendid palomino mare, with an old-fashioned Spanish-type saddle.

He swept off his hat and she flashed a quick smile at him.

"You are Rowdy Horn?" she inquired.

"That's right, ma'am, but you've sure got the best of me. I thought I knew every girl in this country, and especially all of the pretty ones, but I see I don't."

She laughed. "You wouldn't know me," she said sharply. "I'm Vaho Rainey."

His interest quickened. The whole South Rim country knew about this girl, but she had never been seen around Aragon. The daughter of French and Irish parents, she had been left an orphan when little more than a baby, and brought up by old Cleetus, a wealthy Navaho chieftain. When she was fourteen she had been sent to a convent in New Orleans, and after that had spent some time in New York and Boston before returning to the great old stone house where Cleetus lived.

"Welcome to the Slash Bar," Rowdy said, smiling. "I met old Cleetus once. He's quite a character." He grinned ruefully. "He sure made a fool out of me, one time."

He told her how the old Indian had come to his cabin one miserable wintry night, half frozen and with a broken wrist. His horse had fallen on the ice. Rowdy had not known who he was—just any old buck, he had thought—but he had put Cleetus to bed, set the broken bone, and nursed the old man through the blizzard. Returning to the cabin one day after the storm, he had found the old man gone, and with him a buckskin horse. While the old man was still sick, Rowdy had offered him a blanket and food when he left. These Cleetus had taken.

Over a year later, Rowdy Horn had discovered, quite by accident, the identity of the old man he had befriended. And he had learned that Cleetus was one of the wealthiest sheepmen among the Navahos, and one of the first to introduce Angora goats into the lonely desert land where he lived.

Vaho laughed merrily when she heard the story.

"That's like him. So like him. Did he ever return the horse?"

"No," Rowdy said drily, "he didn't. That was a good horse, too."

"He's a strange man, Rowdy," she said. He was glad, somehow, that Vaho did not stand on ceremony. He liked hearing her call him by his first name.

"Maybe he could use a good man with his flocks," Rowdy suggested, a little bitterly. "I'm sure going to be hunting a job soon."

She looked at him quickly. "But you have this ranch? Is that not enough?"

Rowdy did not know just why he had an impulse to tell this girl, a stranger, his trouble—but he did.

## Chapter 2
### *Jilted—and Glad of It*

Shrugging, Rowdy explained, and Vaho Rainey listened attentively, watching him with her wide dark eyes. She frowned thoughtfully at the receding water.

"There must be a reason for this," she said. "There has always been water here. Never in the memory of the Navaho has this water hole been so low."

"Sure, there's a reason," Rowdy said glumly, "but what is it? Maybe there's somebody takin' water before it gets to this pool, but who and where? I always figured this water came off the Rim, somewhere."

"Or from under it," Vaho said thoughtfully.

That remark made no impression on Rowdy at the moment, although he did recall it later, and wondered what she had meant. Right now, his interest in this tall, dark girl was quickening. There was warmth in her, understanding, and sympathy for his problems—all the things that he had missed in Jenny.

He glanced up suddenly. The sun had slid behind the mountains, and it was growing dark.

"You'd better be getting home!" he warned Vaho. "Riding in the mountains at night is no good."

"Not when you know them as I do," she said, smiling. "Anyway, I've not far to go. Some of our people are camped only a few miles from here. I shall go to them."

When he had watched her ride away into the dusk that lay thick among the dark pines, he swung into the saddle and turned the steeldust down the road home. But he was conscious of a strange excitement, and the memory of that tall, dark girl was like a bright fire in his thoughts. He was remembering the curves of her lips and the way she had moved, how her laughter had sounded an echo in his heart. With a quick start of guilt he realized that in his mind he was being a little disloyal to Jenny. Despite his guilty feeling, though, he would not forget that girl from the canyons, or the strange warmth she had left with him.

He had ridden home and had stripped the saddle from the steeldust, when he heard a man's voice inside the stable. For an instant he hesitated. It was dark inside and he could see nothing. Then he saw a subdued glow, and stepped quickly to the door. "Who's there?" he demanded.

A man who had been kneeling to examine Cub's leg got to his feet. As he stepped out of the door Rowdy Horn could see him plainly—a tall, thin man in a battered hat not of western vintage, and a shabby suit of store clothes.

"How are you?" he said. "I hope you won't think I'm butting in. I stopped to ask for something to eat and a place to sleep, but finding nobody at home, I walked around a little. Then I found your horse with the bad leg. What happened to him?"

"Stepped into a gopher hole. My roping horse. I'd figured on riding him in the rodeo."

"Too bad." The man hesitated. "How about that grub?"

"Sure. Come on up to the house. I haven't eaten myself. You passin' through?"

"Uh-huh. I'm a tramp printer, Neil Rice by name. My doctor told me if I expected to live I'd better get West. I'm not really sick, but he told me that any more of that city air and I would be, so I packed up and started West."

"Broke?"

"I am now. I ran into a poker game back in Dodge,

and I'd played a lot of poker with other printers. Those Dodge people played too fast a game for me."

Rowdy chuckled. "All right, Rice. I know how that is. I'm Rowdy Horn. You hunting a job?"

"Any kind of a job. I know a little about horses, but not much about cattle. And I can cook."

"There's what you need," Rowdy said cheerfully. "Let's see what you can do. I am probably the worst cook who ever died of slow poisoning from his own cookin'. I'd hesitate to ask a stranger to eat it."

Two hours later, with a good dinner behind their belts and pipes lighted, they sat back and stared thoughtfully at the fire. Rowdy by that time knew most of Rice's troubles, and the printer was aware of the precarious situation on the Slash Bar.

"This fellow Luby," Rice said thoughtfully. "Has he always lived around this country?"

"Here, Texas, New Mexico, and California, as far as I know. He seems to know a good bit, though."

"I wouldn't be surprised." Rice hesitated. "Is there any way in which I could get my hands on that deed? And the will? I know a little about such things."

Horn shrugged. "Not that I know of. Maybe I can figure out a way. Why? Are you a lawyer?"

Rice chuckled. "Just a printer, but I know a little about documents. I wouldn't promise anything, but it might be that if the deed was faked and if the will was forged, I could tell. How, I don't know, and I couldn't promise anything. I'd have to examine them, and preferably have them for a while."

"That's tough. Luby wouldn't turn loose of them. We'll see, though, for it's sure an idea." He scowled. "You can't forge a deed, can you? This one's got a big seal on it. I gave up when I saw that."

"Well," Rice said, "that might be the very reason it's on there. Did you have a good lawyer look at it?"

"Lawyer?" Horn exclaimed. "Man, there's no lawyer in Aragon but old Hemingway, and he's drunk most of the time. I don't think he knows much law, anyway."

The following day, Rowdy worked hard, roping and tying calves, roping horses, and attempting to improve his own speed and skill, though the steeldust wasn't nearly the horse Cub was. Neil Rice had taken right hold, had cleaned out the house and organized the cooking situation. Then he had handed Horn a list of supplies. Rowdy had grinned at it.

"All right, Rice," he had said, "I reckon we might as well eat and leave this place on full stomachs anyway. I'll head into Aragon and pick up this stuff."

With a packhorse Rowdy Horn headed for Aragon. All the way to town he was studying ways and means of getting the documents into his hands once more. There must be some way. During their talk at breakfast Rice had told him that it was often possible to move a seal from one document to another, that such a thing had been done in more than one place.

Aragon was crowded when Rowdy rode down the main one of the town's three streets. Banners were hanging across the street, and the town was bright with posters heralding the coming Stockman's Show and Rodeo. News had got around about the injury to Cub's leg, however, and everywhere he went he found the odds of his winning first money had dropped. He was no longer given an even chance to win, for everyone had known how much trust he placed in Cub, and all had seen the horse perform at one time or another.

He called at the house for Jenny, but she was out. Her mother smiled at him, but her eyes looked as if she were disturbed.

"I'm sorry, Rowdy," Mrs. Welman told him, "Jenny's gone out. You may see her downtown."

He walked back down the street, telling himself that he was foolish to feel irritated. Jenny had had no idea he would be coming in, and there was no reason why she should be at home. He laughed at himself, then strode back downtown and went to the Emporium, where he began buying groceries. He was packing them on his lead horse when he heard a familiar voice and, glancing up, saw Bart Luby. Clinging to his arm was Jenny Welman!

Rowdy's face flushed, and he looked away, but not before Luby had seen him.

"How are you, Horn?" Bart said, making no effort to conceal his triumph. "Sorry to hear about Cub! I was looking forward to the chance of beating him."

Jenny looked at Rowdy, paling slightly. His eyes met hers for an instant and then he looked away.

"Think nothing of it, Luby," he said, "but don't count me out. I'll be there yet."

"A man can't do much good on just a fair horse," Luby said, "but come along in. Be glad to have you."

Jenny hesitated. "I didn't know you were coming to town," she said.

"I see you didn't," he said, a little wryly.

Her chin lifted and her eyes blazed. "Well, what do you expect me to do? Stay home all the time? Anyway," she added suddenly, "I'd been planning to ride out and see you. I don't think—well, we'd better call this off. Our engagement, I mean."

He had a queer sinking feeling, but when he lifted his eyes, they revealed nothing. "All right," was all he said, calmly.

Her blue eyes hardened slightly. "You certainly don't seem much upset!" she flared.

"Should I be?" he asked. "When a girl tosses a man over the first time he gets in a tight spot, she's small loss."

"Well!" she flared. "I—!"

"Come on, Jenny," Bart said. "You told me you were comin' out to my place to look at the sorrel mare." He grinned at Horn. "Out to the Bar O."

Stung, Rowdy glared at Luby.

"Better enjoy the Bar O while you can, Bart," he said.

Bart Luby froze in midstride and for a second stood stock-still. Then slowly he turned, his face livid. "What do you mean by that?" he barked.

"Nothing"—Rowdy grinned—"nothing at all! Only—" He hesitated, then shrugged. "You'll know all about it soon."

"Oh"—Jenny tugged at Bart's arm—"don't pay any attention to him. He's always fussing about that ranch."

The remark was intended to appease Bart and get him away. It had the effect of adding fuel to the man's uncertainty after Rowdy's veiled comment. Bart Luby stared down at Rowdy as he stood in the street, and watched him finish his diamond hitch.

"If you're smart, you'll leave well enough alone!" Bart said then, carefully and coldly.

Rowdy smiled, but he felt warm with triumph. Luby was worried, and if that deal had been straight, why should he worry? His sudden remark had brought a greater reaction than he had expected, yet suddenly he was aware of something else. That had been a dangerous thing for him to say, for now Luby knew that the loss of the ranch was not a closed matter to Rowdy Horn.

In the saddle on the way back to the Slash Bar, Horn began to feel the letdown. Despite his immediate reaction to Jenny's sudden breaking off of their engagement, and despite the fact that he realized she was small loss, he felt sick and empty inside. He felt so low that he took no notice of the ride he had always loved. The great wall of the Rim did not draw his eyes, nor did the towering mass of cumulus that lifted above it, nor the darkening fringe of the pines against the distant sky.

When he got back home none of his problems were any nearer a solution either. Cub's leg was but little better, and there was absolutely no chance of his recovering before the rodeo date. And more than ever now, Rowdy wanted to win that first place.

Again and again he studied the situation, comparing his own ability with that of Luby, who would be the main competitor. Each time, it all came down to the roping event. A lot would depend, of course, on the kind of mounts each of them drew in the bucking events, but there was little to choose between the two men. To give the devil his due, Bart Luby was a hand.

# Chapter 3
## Girl of the Wilds

At daylight Rowdy Horn was out looking at Cub's leg. When he had done that, he saddled a powerful black for a ride out to the Point of Rocks. Today he must try to find out what was wrong with his water supply. He could delay no longer. He was just cinching the saddle tight when he heard a rattle of hoofs and looked up to see Vaho Rainey sweep into the yard.

His face broke into a smile. This morning the girl was riding a blood bay, a splendid horse. She reined in, swung down, and walked over to him with a free-swinging stride that he liked.

"Rowdy," she asked excitedly, "did you ever hear of Silverside?"

"Silverside?" He looked at her curiously. "Who hasn't? The greatest roping horse this country ever saw, I reckon. Buck Gordon rode him and trained him, and Buck was a roper. There will never be a greater horse."

"Could you win that rodeo on him?"

He laughed. "Could I? On *that* horse? Vaho, I could win anything on that horse. He had the speed of a deer and was smarter than most men. I saw him once, several years ago, before he was killed. He was the finest roping horse I ever saw, and Buck the greatest hand."

"He's not dead, Rowdy. He's alive, and I know where he is."

Rowdy Horn's heart missed a beat. "You aren't foolin'? This isn't a joke?" He shook his head. "It couldn't be Silverside," he protested, "and if you've heard it is, somebody is mistaken. Buck Gordon was riding Silverside when the Apaches got him down near Animas—in one of their last raids over the border. They killed Silverside at the same time. A long time after that somebody found his skeleton, some of the hide, and Buck's saddle."

"He's alive, Rowdy!" Vaho repeated earnestly. "I know where he is, I tell you! Some Mexican picked up Buck's saddle, and when he was killed later, riding a paint, it was that horse that was found, or it must have been. Silverside was taken by the Apaches and they have him now."

Horn shook his head. "It couldn't be, Vaho. The Apaches are at least pretendin' to be friendly now, and have been for a long time. If they had that horse, somebody would have seen him." His eyes sparkled. "Man, I wish they had! With that horse I could sure make Luby back up! There never was a great roper without a great horse, and don't you forget it!"

"You said the Apaches were friendly," said Vaho. "All of them are not."

"Oh? You mean old Cochino? No, he sure isn't. But if that horse was alive and old Cochino had him, I'd still be out of luck. In the first place, nobody knows where he and his renegades hang out, and in the second place, it would be like committing suicide to look for him—if you found him."

"You wouldn't try it?" she persisted. "Not even for Silverside?"

"You bet I would!" Rowdy stated emphatically. "I'd ride through perdition in a celluloid collar for that horse!"

Vaho laughed, and her eyes were bright. "All right, put on your celluloid collar! I know where Cochino is, and I *know* he has Silverside!"

"If you mean that—"

Rowdy hesitated, thinking rapidly. She was positive, and after all, there had long been rumors of a friendship between old Cochino and Cleetus. The Navahos and the Apaches had never been too friendly, but the two old chiefs had found something in common. In fact, it had long been rumored that if Cleetus wanted to, he could tell where Cochino was at any time. But that was just cow-country gossip, and nobody was really looking for the tough and wily old Apache any longer.

"Yes," Rowdy said finally, "if you're positive, Vaho, I'll take a chance. Tell me where he is."

"I can't," Vaho said quietly, "but I'll take you there. But let me warn you—it's an awful ride."

"*You'll* take me there?" He was incredulous. "Nothing doing! I'd take a chance on Cochino myself, but not you!"

"Without me you wouldn't have a chance, Rowdy. With me, you may have. It's a big gamble, for old Cochino is peculiar and uncertain. He still believes the soldiers are after him, and he and the twenty or so renegade Apaches he has with him are dangerous. But he knows me, and he likes old Cleetus. Will you chance it?"

"You're sure you'll be safe?" he protested.

She grew suddenly serious. "I think so, Rowdy. Nobody knows about Cochino. He's like a tiger out of the jungle, one that has been partly trained. He may be all right, and he might turn ugly. But I'm willing to chance it. I want to see you win this rodeo, and I want to see you keep your ranch!"

He looked at her strangely, and as he looked into

the soft depths of those lovely dark eyes, he remembered the momentary hardness of Jenny's blue eyes. Suddenly he knew that Jenny would never have ridden with him in that weird, sun-stricken desert where the Apache lived. Aside from the danger, she would have shied at the discomfort.

Scarcely were Rowdy and Vaho on the trail when doubts began to assail him. The horse Cochino had simply couldn't be Silverside—and it had probably been years since he had been used for roping. Besides, the horse would be ten or eleven years old! Perhaps older. He scowled and mopped his brow, then glanced at the girl riding at his side, her eyes on the horizon.

The devil with it! If he found no horse, if he lost the ranch, if he couldn't beat Luby, the ride with this girl would be worth any chance he took. . . .

Back on the ranch, alone in the cabin, Neil Rice finished cleaning up and put away the dishes. There was work to do outside, but he felt in no mood for it. Idly, he began to rummage around the house, hunting for something to read. The few books failed to strike his interest, but when he was about to give up he remembered having seen several books in an old desk and bookcase in the inner room.

He found them and studied them thoughtfully, one by one. He was about to replace the last one, when he noticed what appeared to be a thin crack in the walnut of the old desk. Curious, he ran his hand back into the space from which he had taken the book. It was then that he noticed, on closer inspection, that there seemed to be some waste space in the desk, or some unaccounted-for space.

Remembering that many such old secretaries or cabinets had secret compartments, he felt around with his fingers, finally dug his nails into the crack, and pulled. The wood moved under his hand, and a small panel slid back!

In the small space beyond, he felt several pieces of paper. One had the feel of parchment. Slowly, he got his fingers on them and drew them out, then took them to the window for better light.

The first was an old legal paper, a corporate charter of some long-defunct mining company. What caught his eye at once was the missing seal. His eyes narrowed thoughtfully. Then he opened the next paper. Glancing at the heading, he read:

LAST WILL AND TESTAMENT OF
THOMAS B. SLATER

His eyes sharpening, he read on:

I, Thomas B. Slater, being of sound mind, make this my last will and testament. After payment of my just debts and funeral expenses, I devise and bequeath all my worldly goods and properties to Rowell D. Horn, who has been as a son to me through many months and whose friendship and interest in the future and well-being of the Bar O have shown him a fit person to possess this property.

There was more, and it was followed by the signature of the old rancher and that of two witnesses. Rice had never heard of either of them. He studied the document for a long time, then closed the compartment and replaced the book. He retained the charter with the missing seal and the will.

"Now wouldn't Bart Luby like to know about *this*!" he muttered thoughtfully.

He scowled. Possibly Luby *did* know about it. Hadn't Rowdy said that this place had been for a long time a line cabin for the Bar O? And after that for a while it had been headquarters for Bart Luby's cattle buying. No doubt Luby had taken the seal from this document, and then had concealed it and the will, believing that he might have some further use for it, at least for the signature; so he had hidden the will until he could make up his mind. He might have expected the place to be in his possession longer than it had been, but when Rowdy Horn had made his down payment without Luby's knowledge and had appeared suddenly and unexpectedly to take over, it may have left no chance for Luby to get into the old cabinet—until he could slip back secretly. And he had probably believed it safely hidden.

That the will was in existence at all was a serious oversight on Luby's part. Once in his hands, he should have destroyed it. Here, Rice thought, was the key to the whole situation in South Rim. With this, Rowdy could get the Bar O and prove that Luby was the crook Rowdy believed him to be. But suppose Luby got it? There might be a lot of money in these papers if handled discreetly.

Neil Rice was painfully conscious of the emptiness of his own pockets. He came to a decision suddenly. He would ride into Aragon. . . .

Out on the range with Rowdy Horn, Vaho Rainey led the way, and the route she took led across the wide sagebrush flats toward the vague purple of distant mountains. Before they had ridden a mile they seemed lost in a limitless sea of distance where they moved at the hub of an enormous wheel of mountains. They talked but little, riding steadily onward into the morning sunlight, but Rowdy Horn kept his mind on the slim, erect girl who rode sometimes before him and sometimes behind.

As they drew nearer the mountains beyond the wide disk of the desert, Rowdy could see that what had appeared to be a wall of purple was actually broken into weird figures and towers, strange, grotesque monsters sculptured from the sandstone by sun, wind, and rain. The trail led along the valley floor between these rows of columns or battlemented walls, the sagebrush fell behind, and there was mesquite, a sure sign of under-surface water.

The afternoon was spent among the columns of sandstone and granite, then Vaho guided Rowdy into what was scarcely more than a crease between rolling hills. A mile of this and it widened, and they went down through a forest of saguaro. Then the trail wound steeply up among towering crags, and the saguaro was left behind, traded by the trail for borders of piñon and juniper. Some of their squat, gnarled trunks seemed gray with age and wind, but the bright green of their foliage was a vivid, living streak across the reds and pinks of the Kaibab sandstone.

Yellow tamarisks, smoke trees, and orange-hued rabbit brush brightened the way, but the mountains became more lonely. As dusk drew on they rounded into a small basin, grass floored and cool, and here Vaho swung down. For all the heat and the length of the ride, she appeared fresh. "We'll camp here," she said, indicating the water hole.

"All night?" he asked.

She looked at him and smiled lightly. "Of course. The devil himself couldn't travel by night where we're going."

"You aren't afraid?" he asked curiously. "I mean, well—you don't know me very well, do you?"

"No, I'm not afraid. Should I be?"

He shrugged, not knowing whether to be pleased or deflated.

"No, of course not," he said.

There was plenty of dry wood, bone dry and dusty, most of it. In a few minutes he had wood gathered and a fire going. He picketed the horses while Vaho began to prepare food. He watched her thoughtfully.

"You're quite a girl, you know," he said suddenly.

She laughed. "Why did you think I started this if it wasn't to show you that?" she asked. "I'm not a town girl, Rowdy. I could never be. Not all the time I was away at school, nor in all my traveling to New Orleans or New York or Boston did I ever forget the desert."

"I'm glad," he said, although he knew as he spoke that he was not quite sure why he should be glad. So he added lamely, "Some man is going to get a fine girl. He'll be lucky!"

She looked at him thoughtfully, then lifted the coffee from the fire.

"He will be if he likes the desert and mountains," was her only comment.

When they had finished eating he threw more wood on the fire and stretched out on the sand where he could look across the flames into Vaho's eyes. He felt vastly comfortable and relaxed, with myriad stars littered across the sky. The black loom of the cliffs, the ranch, the rodeo, and even Jenny seemed far behind.

They talked for a long time, while in the distance a coyote yapped at the stars. The grass rustled softly with the movements of the horses as they cropped quietly of the rich green grass.

# Chapter 4
## *Silverside*

Daybreak found Rowdy and Vaho moving again, and dipping down into the wide white bowl of another arm of the desert. Sweat broke out on Rowdy's forehead as the heat waves banked higher around them. There was no air, no movement save their own, and always and forever the heat.

Suddenly, Vaho Rainey turned her bay at right

angles and dipped steeply down a narrow path to the bottom of a great sink. It was at least a thousand yards across, and all of two hundred feet from bottom to rim. Against the far wall, walled in by a huddle of stones, was a pool of clear cold water, and the dozen or so wickiups of Cochino, the Apache chief.

Rowdy Horn's pulse leaped as he saw the horses scattered nearby, feeding quietly, for among them was the tall black horse with the single great splash of white upon his left side—Silverside, the greatest roping horse he had ever seen!

His eyes turned again to the village. Nobody was in sight, neither squaws nor children, but he was conscious of watching eyes. For years the old renegade Apache had refused to live on a reservation, instead retreating steadily into the farthest vastnesses of the desert and mountains. At times he had fought savagely, but in the last years he had merely held to his loneliness, fiercely resenting any attempt to come near him or lure him out. It was reported that his braves were insane, that he was mad, that they had eaten of the fruit of a desert plant that rendered them all as deadly as marihuana addicts.

Vaho drew rein. "Be very careful, Rowdy," she said, low voiced. "Make no quick moves, and let me do the talking."

From behind the wickiups and out of the rocks the Indians began to appear. Attired only in the skimpiest of breechclouts, their dusky bodies were dark as some of the burnt red rocks of the desert, and looked as rough as old lava. Their black eyes looked hard as flint, as one by one they came down from the rocks and slowly gathered in a circle about the two riders.

Rowdy could feel his heart pounding, and was conscious of the weight of the six-shooter against his leg. It would be nip and tuck if anything started here. He might get a few of them, but they would get him in the end. Suddenly he cursed himself for a fool for having come here or letting Vaho come.

An old man emerged from the group and stared at them with hard, unblinking eyes. Vaho suddenly started to speak. Knowing a few words of Apache, Rowdy could follow her conversation. She was explaining that she was the adopted daughter of Cleetus, that he sent his best wishes to Cochino, the greatest of all Apache war chiefs.

The old man stared at her, then at Rowdy. His reply Horn could not interpret, but Vaho said to Rowdy suddenly, "He says for us to get down. He will talk."

That was no proof of their safety, yet it was something. Rowdy swung down and allowed an Indian to take their horses, then he followed Cochino to the fire, and all seated themselves. After a few minutes the girl took some of the presents they had brought from the bag she had prepared with Rowdy's help. A fine steel hunting knife, a package of tobacco, a bolt of red calico, other presents.

Cochino looked at them, but his expression was bleak. He lifted his eyes to Vaho, and there was a question in them. Slowly, she began to explain. This friend—she gestured to Rowdy—was the friend of Cleetus also. She told how he had taken the old Indian in, treated his broken arm, fed him and cared for him until he was able to move. She explained how Rowdy was a great warrior, but that in the games of his people he could not compete because his horse was injured, that he was an unhappy man. Then she had told him that her friend Cochino, the friend also of Cleetus, had a magnificent horse that he might lend or sell—the great Silverside.

For an hour the talk went on. Following it with difficulty, Rowdy Horn could be sure of nothing. Cochino should have been a poker player, he reflected. His expression was unreadable. Little by little, however, he seemed to be showing approval of Rowdy, and of Vaho.

Suddenly he asked a question, looking from Rowdy to the girl, and she flushed.

Rowdy glanced at her quickly. "What did he want to know?" he said.

She would not meet his eyes, but continued to talk. He listened, straining his ears to get every syllable, doing his best to interpret what she was saying. The old Apache suddenly chuckled. It was a grim, hard sound, but there was a glint of ironic humor in his eyes as he looked from the girl to Rowdy. Finally, he nodded.

"Yes," he said, speaking plainly in English.

Her face flushed with happiness, Vaho turned to Rowdy, putting her hand impulsively on his arm.

"He says you can have the horse! He gives him to you, and he wishes you luck."

The old Indian got to his feet, and they did also.

"Tell him," Rowdy said impulsively, "that when he wishes, if there is anything a friend can do for him or his people, to come to me, or to send a messenger. There is only peace and brotherhood between the people of Cochino and Rowdy Horn."

She explained briefly, and the old Indian nodded gravely.

"Invite him to the rodeo if he wishes to come," Rowdy added.

Vaho spoke swiftly, and the old Indian stared at them, his eyes bleak. Then he shook his head.

"He says," Vaho explained, "he is too old to give up now. As he has lived, so will he die."

A long time after that, riding away through the great broken hills, Rowdy glanced back again and again at the splendid horse he was leading. And that night when they camped again beside the pool, he talked with the tall horse, curried him carefully. The horse nuzzled him, eager for affection.

Vaho walked out to them from the fire, and he looked around at her. "This horse is almost human," he said. "Somehow he gives a man the feeling of standing near something superb, something beyond just horse-flesh."

She nodded. "I know. He likes you too, Rowdy. Already that is plain." She hesitated for a moment. "But Rowdy, it has been a long time since he has worked with cattle. Do you think he will be as good?"

"I've no idea," he admitted, "but he's my only chance, and somehow I think we'll make it. Anyway, it will be a treat to ride this horse."

Yet he was scarcely thinking of that. He was thinking of the girl by his side—tall, clean limbed, and lovely—and he was remembering the long ride through the desert beside her, the calm way she had talked to Cochino, the strange feeling of ease and happiness he had when riding with her, when knowing she was close to him. She was in his thoughts even as he slept—and dreamed. . . .

"Rowdy," Vaho said suddenly the following morning, "there's another trail, a way through the Rim to the back of your place. Old Cleetus showed it to me when I was just a little girl. Let's go that way. I think it's shorter."

Turning their horses they cut off through the pines toward the blue haze that hung in the distance, and abruptly they drew up on the very edge of an amazing canyon whose sides dropped sheer away to the sandy bottom where a small stream slid over a bottom now of rocks, now of sand. Skirting the cliff, they came to a steep path and wound their way down. When they and their horses had rested and had drunk long of the clear, cold water, they mounted again and turned downstream.

It was cool in the shadow of the cliffs. When they had followed the canyon for several hours, Rowdy called softly to Vaho, who had ridden on ahead.

"Look here." He drew up, pointing.

In the sand of the canyon bottom were the tracks of several shod horses.

"No Indian ponies," he said grimly, "and no white man that I know of knows this country. Except one."

"You think it's Rollick?" she asked.

"Who else? Times have changed since the old days, but there's still a market for rustled beef, and Jack Rollick is supposed to be back in here somewhere."

"The tracks go the same way we're going," she said, "but there's no way out of here now except downstream."

"Let's go," he said grimly.

He reached back and slipped the thong from the butt of his six-gun. His rifle he always carried in a scabbard that pointed forward and down just ahead of his right knee so that the stock of the rifle was within easy grasp of his right hand. He was glad now that it was so handy.

Riding cautiously downstream they had gone no more than two miles when suddenly the canyon widened out and the rock walls fell back. They drew up sharply in the screen of aspen and willow beside the trail. Before them was a wide green meadow through which coursed the stream. The meadow was all of fifty acres in extent. A branch canyon seemed to lead off an immeasurable distance to the right. Within view were at least one hundred head of cattle, fattening on the grass.

Beyond, and close to the sheer wall at the far end of the little meadow, was a stone cabin, and a corral. There were several horses in the corral. No saddled horses were in sight.

Skirting the cliff wall, they circled to the right, trusting to the sparse trees and the brush, as well as to the wide shadow of the encircling cliffs, to hide them. As they neared the cabin, Rowdy saw that the stream had been dammed and there was a large pool, all of an acre in extent.

Vaho touched his arm, indicating the pool. "That may be your trouble," she said, low voiced. "This stream is probably the source of your water supply."

He had been thinking the same thing, and he nodded. When they had a better view, he could see that no more than a trickle seemed to be escaping from the pool, and the waters of the stream had been diverted to irrigate another small meadow.

More cattle were in view in the branch canyon. Rowdy Horn estimated that three hundred head were held here. From the brands he saw, nearly every ranch in the South Rim country was represented except the Bar O. That was, in itself, evidence of a kind. He stored the fact grimly away in his mind.

"Nobody around," he said thoughtfully. "I'm going to have a look in that cabin."

"I'll wait here," Vaho said. "Be careful."

He left her with Silverside and rode forward slowly. When near the cabin he dismounted and walked nearer on cat feet. A glance through the window showed the cabin to be empty. Stepping inside, he took a hasty look around. Six or seven men were bunking here, and they had supplies and ammunition enough to last a long time. Also, the house gave every evidence of long occupancy.

Under one of the bunks he saw a square black box and drew it out. It was padlocked, but picking up a hatchet, he smashed the lock with a few well-directed blows. Inside the box were a couple of engraved six-shooters, some odds and ends of letters addressed to Jack Rollick, and a small black tally book. He had picked it up and opened it, when he heard a scream.

With a lunge he was on his feet, racing to the door. He sprang outside, his eyes swinging to the woods where he had left Vaho. The bushes were thrashing, and he heard another low cry. Instantly he vaulted into saddle and the black horse lunged into a dead run for the woods. Rowdy hit the ground running, and dived through the bushes.

Vaho, her blouse torn, was fighting desperately with a tall, powerful man in a sweat-stained red shirt. When Rowdy plunged through the brush, the man's head turned. With an oath he hurled the girl from him and grabbed for his gun.

His draw was like a flash of light, and in an instant of desperation as the big man's hand darted, Rowdy Horn knew he could never match that draw, yet he palmed his own gun. The rustler's six-shooter roared, then Rowdy fired.

The big man lifted on his tiptoes, raised his eyebrows, and opened his mouth slowly, then plunged over on his face.

# Chapter 5
## *Framed into Jail*

Carefully, gun ready, Rowdy walked forward. He had never killed a man before, and he was frightened. The rustler's shot had been hasty and had missed. Evidently, the big fellow had stumbled when he tried to move, for Rowdy's bullet had gone into his back, just behind his left arm, and had come out under the heart.

"Oh, Rowdy!" Vaho cried, her eyes wide. "You killed him!"

"I reckon I did!" he said. "And I reckon we'd better make tracks out of here before they get back! There's at least five or six more of them around somewhere."

Swiftly they rode away, and in his hip pocket was the black tally book, forgotten.

They were skirting the Slash Bar range when Vaho

spoke up suddenly. "Rowdy, hadn't you better ride on into Aragon and report this to the sheriff? Wouldn't it be best?"

"That's a good idea," he said worriedly. "What about you?"

"I'll wait at the Point of Rocks with Silverside. You can cut across to town; then come back here and we'll go on to your place."

Despite the fact that the killing had been in self-defense, and to protect Vaho, Rowdy was worried. It was no small thing to kill a man, even a thief and rustler. He rode swiftly, hurrying by every shortcut he knew, for Aragon. Yet when he arrived, the sheriff's office was deserted. He walked down the street, but could find him nowhere.

Eager to be back with Vaho, and worried about her—for he realized that the dead rustler's friends might trail them—Rowdy finally abandoned his quest for the sheriff and returned to the Point of Rocks. Together they rode on to the Slash Bar.

Riding into the yard, he called out, but there was no reply. Neil Rice was evidently away. Rowdy swung down, and wearily the girl dismounted. He stripped the saddles and bridles from the sweat-stained horses and turned all three of them into the corral. He and Vaho walked toward the house, but Vaho halted suddenly.

"Rowdy," she said, "I'm as tired as can be, but I should be going back to the Indians. Cleetus was to come today, and he'll be worried about me."

"All right." He turned back and saddled a paint horse for her to ride. As she sat in the saddle, he took her hand. "Vaho," he said, "you've been swell. I didn't know they made them like you."

"It's all right. I liked doing it."

"Look," he said. "After the rodeo there's a big dance. Will you go with me?"

Her eyes brightened. "Oh, Rowdy! I'd love to! A

dance! Why, I haven't danced since I left Boston! Of course I'll go!"

When she was out of sight in the gathering dusk, he turned back again toward the cabin. Opening the door, he walked in. The place was hot and stuffy, so he left the door open. Striking a match, he lit the coal-oil lamp, then turned around to replace it in the bracket. With the lamp in his hand, he stopped, riveted to the spot.

There on the floor of his cabin lay the body of a dead man. The red-shirted man he had killed at the hideout!

But how on earth had he come here? Rowdy did not even hear the approaching horses until a voice spoke abruptly behind him: "Here! What's this?"

Turning, he found Sheriff Ben Wells staring from him to the body.

"What's happened here?" demanded the lawman. "Who is this hombre?"

Behind Wells was Bart Luby and Mike McNulty. "That's cold-blooded killing, Ben!" Luby said triumphantly. "This man was shot in the back."

"He was not!" Horn declared hotly. "He was left side toward me, and he fired, then started to move. My bullet went in where you see it, back of his arm."

"It's still in his back!" Luby said. "And," he added grimly, "we have only your story for it. You say he fired a shot. Why, his gun's still in its holster!"

"He wasn't killed here!" Horn said angrily. "This hombre grabbed Vaho Rainey when we were riding back of the Rim. I rushed up to help and he drew and fired. He missed and I shot and killed him!"

Sheriff Wells knelt beside the body. Drawing the gun, he checked it, then looked up, his face grave.

"This gun is fully loaded," he said, "and hasn't been fired!"

"What?" Rowdy was dumbfounded. "Why, that couldn't be. He—" He shrugged. "Well, I reckon the man or men who brought him here changed guns with him."

Wells gnawed at his gray mustache. Secretly, he had always liked Rowdy Horn as much as he disliked Bart Luby, but this story was out of all reason.

"You mean to say," he demanded, "that you killed this man back of the Rim? And that somebody packed his carcass down here and dumped him on you?"

"That's exactly what happened!" Rowdy Horn said flatly. "It's the only way it could have happened."

Luby laughed. "Give him credit for being original, Ben. But he certainly hasn't much respect for your intelligence, to try a story like that."

"You'll have to come into town, son," Wells said, his voice hardening. "This will have to be explained."

"But you can't put me in jail!" Rowdy pleaded. "Think, man! The rodeo's tomorrow."

"You should have thought of that," Luby suggested, "before you killed this man. Anyway, that's no excuse. Your ropin' horse is laid up, so you can't compete!"

On the verge of bursting out with an explanation about Silverside, he caught himself just in time. If he had to go to jail, and there was nobody to watch the horse, it might easily be stolen.

"I knew this hombre," McNulty said suddenly. "He was Jake Leener, one of the Rollick outfit."

"No matter," Wells said positively. "He was shot in the back. We had nothing against him, even if he did ride with Rollick. The law can't call a man a crook until he's known to be one. This here hombre hadn't no record I know of, and he sure ain't wanted now."

"But listen!" Rowdy protested. "I've a witness! Vaho Rainey saw all this! She knows what happened!"

"Vaho Rainey?" Wells stared at him. "Rowdy, what you giving us? If that girl was with you, where is she now? You know as well as I do that if there is any such girl nobody has seen her around. You're just pullin' rabbits out of your hat. Tell us what happened, and I'll see you get a break if you've got one comin'."

"I told you what happened!" Horn said stubbornly. "Take it or leave it!"

"We'll take you," Wells said. "Mike, rustle this gent's horse, and be quick!"

Bart Luby glanced thoughtfully across the room toward the door of the bedroom. He was thinking of that old cabinet. Now that he was arrested, Horn would be away from the house. In the dozen or so times he had tried to enter, he had failed to find him away even once. But with a killer charge hanging over him he would not return, and he was out of the rodeo. . . .

It was a solemn and silent group that rode over the trail to Aragon. Grimly, Rowdy thought that this was the last straw. He was through now. The rodeo had been his last hope. With that money, even though he had lost Jenny, he could pay off the mortgage on his ranch.

His thought of Jenny brought it home to him that he had scarcely thought of her for days. Ever since he had first seen her, several years before, he had dreamed of her. She had been an ideal girl, the prettiest one around, and all his attentions had been centered upon her. When they had become engaged, it was almost more than he could believe.

Yet after he had begun to see more of her and know her better, his first doubts of her had arisen. After all, there were other things than beauty, and although he told himself he was being unjust, Jenny seemed to be lacking in too many of them. Despite this, his loyalty made him refuse to accept the evidence of his senses until the day she had broken their engagement. For in spite of the shock and pain of that moment, he had felt a queer sense of escape and relief.

In town Rowdy was safely lodged in jail, and the morning sun was making a latticework of bars on the wall opposite the cell window when he awakened with a start. For an instant he lay still, then it hit him, and his heart went sick. After all his planning, he was stuck in jail on the day of the rodeo!

He got up slowly, dressed, and splashed his face in the bucket of cold water that had been left for him. Gloomily he stared out of the barred window at the crowded streets. Already the hitching rails were lined with horses, and there were many buckboards and spring wagons in town. In another hour the streets would be jammed. It began to look as if the boosters of Aragon and the annual Stockman's Show and Rodeo would be right: that between two and three thousand spectators would be on hand for the show.

Yet as he paced the floor, cursing his luck and alternately staring out the window and going to the barred door, hours passed. He heard the band playing, and the confusion that heralded the big parade that opened the rodeo. And then suddenly Sheriff Ben Wells was at the bars.

"Rowdy, if I turn you loose to compete in this show, will you promise not to leave town?" Wells gnawed at his mustache. "I know you, son, and I never figured you'd shoot a man in the back, but that story of yours is plumb farfetched. But just now I got a lead that may help. Maybe we jumped to conclusions, so I'm goin' to turn you loose for the duration of the rodeo."

With a whoop of joy, Horn jumped to the opening door. Grabbing the sheriff's hand, he tried to thank him, but Wells shook his head.

"Don't thank me. Thank this young lady here."

Rowdy turned quickly to face Vaho Rainey.

"You? You got here?"

"You invited me for the dance. Have you forgotten?" She laughed. "When I heard you were in jail, naturally I had to get you out! A girl can't go to a dance with a man who's in jail, can she, Sheriff?"

Ben Wells shook his head, his eyes twinkling. "Son," he said seriously, "I don't know where you found her or how you rate it, but you've got a wonderful girl there, and I'd sure latch on to her if I was you."

Vaho reddened, but her eyes were bright. She was still wearing her denims and blue shirt, but she was sparkling this morning. Rowdy took her arm and squeezed it.

"How in the world did you do it?" he exclaimed.

"I'll tell you later. Only it wasn't just what I did. Now we have to get down to the rodeo grounds. Silverside is down there, waiting for you. We've covered him with a blanket so nobody will know who he is."

Vaho had thought of everything, Rowdy found. Mike McNulty had rousted out the outfit Rowdy had purchased to wear in the rodeo, and in a short time Rowdy had bathed and changed. He came out, immaculate in dove-gray shirt and trousers, with a white hat and a black neckerchief. Black braid outlined his pockets. He wore his guns, but in new holsters, black and shining. His boots, which he had been breaking in around the ranch, felt good.

Vaho's eyes widened. "Why, Rowdy!" she exclaimed. "You're handsome!"

He blushed. "Me?" he choked. And as Mike McNulty and Pete Chamberlain went into roars of laughter, he flushed even deeper.

Hurriedly, he rushed over to Silverside and stripped the blanket from the horse. After a brief workout with the animal, he brought him back to the stall they had procured for him.

"Don't let anybody near him," he warned. "All I'll have to do on that horse is throw the rope! He's so smart he scares me!"

## Chapter 6
### Devil May Care

With Vaho at his side, Rowdy turned toward the arena. The stands were jammed. Going through the gate toward the chutes, almost the first person Rowdy saw was Bart Luby. And with him was Jenny Welman!

Bart started and scowled. "What are you doin' out?" he demanded.

Jenny's eyes had gone immediately to the girl, taking in Vaho's shabby outdoor clothes with a quick contemptuous smile.

"I'm ridin' in the show, Bart," Rowdy drawled. "Reckon you'll have me to beat, ropin' and everything."

"Where'd you get a horse?" Luby demanded suspiciously.

"I've got one." Rowdy's eyes shifted to Jenny. Suddenly he was no longer angry or even irritated with her. "Jenny," he said pleasantly, "I want you to know Vaho Rainey. Miss Rainey, Miss Welman and Bart Luby."

"Oh!" Jenny exclaimed. "You're that Indian girl, aren't you? Or a white girl who lives down in the wickiups? I've forgotten which."

"Yes, that's who I am," Vaho said easily, and Rowdy grinned at the quick smile on her lips. It wouldn't be necessary to protect Vaho, he could see. The contempt in Jenny's voice had been evident, as was the malice, but Vaho was equal to it. "And it's nice to be here today," Vaho added.

"It must be," Jenny fired back. "I hear it's very dirty down there, and it would be a relief to get away for a while."

"Any change is a relief," Vaho replied gently. "You should try it sometime, or"—her voice was suddenly level—"would you rather continue to be a girl of the town?"

Before Jenny, whose face went white with fury, could reply, Vaho took Rowdy's arm.

"Shall we go, dear?" she said sweetly.

As they strolled away, Jenny got her voice back. "Girl of the town!" she cried furiously. "Why, that no-account Indian! I could—"

"Forget it!" Bart said, shrugging. "She just meant you were a city girl."

"I know what she meant!" Jenny flared.

But Luby was not listening. He was staring at his toes, thinking, and his thoughts were not pleasant. In spite of all his plans, Rowdy Horn would ride in the rodeo today, and if Wells had released him, it could only be on sufficient evidence to clear him.

Could it have been the testimony of this girl, Vaho, alone? He weighed that thoughtfully. Doubt arose, for there had been triumph in Rowdy Horn's eyes. Well, no matter. Rowdy had no roping horse, and that was one event he could not hope to win. Nor would he win the bronc riding. For all that, however, Luby's mind was not at ease. There was something wrong, something very wrong, where he was concerned.

As soon as Vaho Rainey and Rowdy reached the chutes, she had excused herself and disappeared. The parade was lining up for the ride around the arena, and McNulty led Silverside, saddled, but still under a blanket, up to where Rowdy Horn was waiting. Beside him was the palomino for Vaho.

The band began to play, and there were excited shouts from the crowd. Silverside's head lifted, and the splendid-appearing horse tossed his head, eyes bright and nostrils distended, as old memories of parades and triumph flooded back. Rowdy stepped to his side.

"Yes, this is it, boy! Show them for me, just like you did for Buck!" The big horse bobbed his head, as if in assent.

Suddenly, Mike let out an awed exclamation. "Boss!" he whispered hoarsely. "Look!"

Startled by McNulty's voice, Rowdy turned, and his mouth dropped open. Before him, resplendent in formfitting forest green and silver, was Vaho Rainey!

Never more beautiful in her life, the tall, dark girl looked proudly into his eyes—proudly, yet hesitantly—looking for the evidence that he found her lovely. And it was there. It was in the eyes of every man who had turned at Mike's astonished exclamation.

Never in all her days had Jenny Welman been as lovely as this. Her pale blond beauty was a poor shadow beside this vivid loveliness, dark, flashing, proud.

"Am I all right?" Vaho asked, her eyes bright with fun. "I had the suit made, and saved it. I knew, somehow, you'd ride. And I wanted you to be proud of me!"

"*Proud* of you?" he shouted. "Honey, I feel like some fairy princess had waved a wand over a little woods girl and turned her into something better than the Queen of Sheba and Helen of Troy rolled into one! Wait till the crowd sees you!"

"Don't you want, just a little," she said gently, "to have Jenny Welman see me?" Her eyes sparkled as she asked the question primly.

He grinned. "I sure do!" he said.

Mike McNulty jerked the blanket from Silverside, and after helping Vaho into the saddle on the palomino, Rowdy Horn swung up himself.

Sheriff Ben Wells walked up with Dick Weaver, the rodeo boss. Weaver froze in midstride.

"Hey!" he shouted. "Ain't that Silverside?"

At the magical name of the greatest rodeo horse of the southwest, men wheeled about. There were shouts, and others came running. They gathered around, staring.

"He's Silverside, all right," Horn said quietly.

Then the band struck up once more, and the parade began to move.

As if by magic that name had flown across the arena, so that by the time the contestants rode into the arena all eyes were turned to find the great horse, so miraculously back from the dead. And the eyes of the crowd went from the great horse to the rider, tall in the saddle, and to the girl in green and silver who rode beside him. Jenny Welman, hearing all the excited talk, turned in her saddle—she was riding beside Luby—and the smile on her face froze. The laughter went out of her. Beside that girl with Rowdy she herself looked shabby and small, and she knew it.

Bart Luby heard the name of Silverside, but would not turn. His heart pounded, and his lips tightened. This rodeo meant more to him than anything in the world, and he was going to win! He was going to win, no matter how!

There was scarcely a person in the crowd but understood what drama and excitement lay before them. Gossip in a small town flies quickly, and the fact that Jenny Welman had returned Rowdy Horn's ring was known to them all, as was the trouble and rivalry between Bart Luby and the young rancher who would ride against him today.

The mysterious girl from the mountains, whom all had heard of but never seen, was before them now, riding proudly beside Rowdy. And to top it all, Rowdy Horn—out of the running when his horse, Cub, had gone lame—had come in at the last minute, freed from jail, to ride. And he was mounted on the greatest horse of the generation—Silverside!

Rowdy Horn watched carefully as he waited beside the chute. There were some good hands riding in this show. Still, he knew, the man he had to beat was Bart Luby.

Never before had he appeared before a crowd of this size. He had been riding all his life, and had appeared in various small-town rodeos, and had spent two summers breaking wild broncs for the rough string. For the sheer sport of it and a little mount money, he had ridden in tryouts when big showmen were testing contest stock for the big shows. But he was in no sense the professional that Luby was.

Roping was his specialty; it was part of his day's work and had been for a long time, but he had never competed in such a show as this, even if it did not rank anywhere near tops in size.

Bart Luby, on the other hand, had been appearing in all the big shows and winning consistently, and he had been competing against the greatest performers in the business. Today, in the first event, the preliminaries in the calf roping, Rowdy would be riding a horse which for all its greatness was unfamiliar to him. Bitterly, he stared out at the dusty arena, soon to be the scene of battle and danger, and for the first time realized what this attempt really meant.

He was no stranger to the flying hoofs and tigerish bucking of outlaw horses or Brahma bulls. He had seen men die in the arena, had seen others crippled or broken under the lashing hoofs of some maddened bronc. But for Rowdy more than life was at stake out there today, and remembering Luby from the old days on the Bar O, he knew the man was fast and skillful. Undoubtedly, he had grown more so.

"I'm a fool," Horn told himself. "I'm bucking a stacked deck. I'm not good enough for these hombres."

After the parade was over, gloomily, Rowdy watched the first leppy dart from the chute and leg it across the arena, with a cowboy on a flying paint horse behind it. That was Gus Petro, a Greek rider from Cheyenne. Doubts lost in sudden interest, Rowdy watched the dust clear, and heard the time called. He smiled. He could beat that. He knew he could beat it.

Yet when the official announcer announced his own name, and he heard that voice rolling out over the arena, something leaped inside him.

"Folks, here comes Rowdy Horn, of the Slash Bar, ridin' that greatest ropin' horse of all time—*Silverside!*"

The calf darted like a creamy streak, and Silverside

took off with a bound. Instantly, Rowdy knew that all he had heard of the horse he bestrode was only half the truth. With flashing speed, the black horse with the splash of white on his side was after the fleeing calf. Horn's rope shot out like an arrow, and in almost the same breath, Rowdy was off the horse, grounding the bawling, struggling calf and making a quick tie. He sprang away from the calf.

"There it is, folks!" Weaver's voice boomed out over the arena. "Eleven seconds even, for Rowdy Horn on Silverside!"

Bart Luby's eyes narrowed. It was a tough mark, yet he had tied it twice. He was off like a streak when his calf darted away from the chute. He roped, flopped the calf, and made his tie.

"Eleven and one-fifth seconds!" Weaver bawled.

Luby swore softly, his eyes bitter. With a jerk he whipped his horse's head around and rode off to the stands. These were only preliminaries, and the final test was yet to be made. But he had never believed that Rowdy Horn would beat him, even by a fifth of a second in a tryout, and he didn't like being beaten.

While the band played and the clowns ripped and tore around the tanbark, mimicking the performances of the preceding event, the contestants headed for the shack to draw horses for the saddle bronc riding contest.

Vaho was waiting for Rowdy near chute 5, from which he would ride. He found that he had drawn Devil May Care, a wicked bucker that had been ridden only twice the preceding year in twenty-two attempts, and not at all in the current season. Bart Luby had drawn an equally bad horse, Firefly.

"You were wonderful!" Vaho said, as Rowdy walked up. "I never saw anyone move so fast!"

He grinned a little. "It's got to be better, honey," he said honestly. "Bart Luby has done that well, and he'll be really trying next time."

"You can do it!" she insisted. "I know you can!"

"Maybe," he said. "But if I do, it will be that horse. I'll know him better next time. Let's just hope I draw a calf that's fast."

"How about this event?" she asked, worriedly. "You drew a bad horse."

"Just what I wanted. You can't win in these rodeos on the easy ones. The worse they buck, the better the ride—if you stay up there."

Bart Luby was first out of the chute on Firefly, and the horse was a demon. It left the chute with a rush and broke into a charge, then swapped ends three times with lightning speed and went into an insane orgy of sunfishing. Luby, riding like the splendid performer he was, raked the big horse fore and aft, writing his name all over its sides with both spurs. At the finish he was still in the saddle and making a magnificent ride. He hopped off and lifted a hand to the cheers of the crowd.

Rowdy stared out through the dust and touched his tongue to dry lips. He mounted the side of the chute and looked down at the trembling body of the sorrel, Devil May Care. Sheriff Ben Wells stood nearby, and he looked up at Horn.

"Watch yourself, boy. This horse is a mean one. When you leave him, don't turn your back or you're a goner."

Rowdy nodded and, tight lipped, lowered himself into the saddle and eased his feet into the stirrups. His fingers took a tighter hold on the reins, and he heard Weaver's voice booming again.

"Here it comes, folks! Right out of chute five! Rowdy Horn on that bundle of pure poison and dynamite, Devil May Care!"

Rowdy removed his hat and yelled, "Let 'er go, boys!"

The gate tripped open and Devil May Care exploded into the arena in a blur of speed and pounding hoofs. His lithe body twisting in unison with the movements of the horse, Rowdy Horn got one frenzied view of the whirling faces of the crowd, then the horse under

him went mad in a series of gyrations and sunfishing
that made anything Rowdy had ever encountered before seem a pale shadow.

The sorrel outlaw was a fighter from way back, and
he knew just exactly why he was out here. He was
going to have this clinging burr out of the saddle or
know the reason why. Devil May Care swallowed his
head and lashed at the clouds with his heels and went
into another hurricane of sunfishing, all four feet spurn-
ing the dust, his whipcord body jackknifing with every
jump. He swapped ends as Rowdy piled up points,
scratching the sorrel with both spurs.

Suddenly, with less than a second to go, the sorrel
raced for the north wall and swung broadside in a
wicked attempt to scrape his rider off. In one grasping
breath, Rowdy saw that the horse was going to miss the
wall by inches. He kept his foot in the stirrup, fighting
the big horse's head around. Devil May Care came
around like the devil he was and, as the whistle sounded,
went into a wicked burst of bucking that made anything
in the past seem mild by comparison.

# Chapter 7
## *Unlisted Event*

Riders rushed from near the judges' stand, and Rowdy
kicked loose both feet and left the horse just as all four
feet of the sorrel hit ground. Wheeling, teeth bared,
Devil May Care sprang for his rider, but the horsemen
wheeled alongside and snared the maddened bronc.
With cheers ringing in his ears, Rowdy Horn walked
slowly back across the arena. The crowd was still cheer-
ing when he walked up to chute 5.

Wells grinned at him. "That horse must be on your
side, son," he said. "Goin' for you like that sure im-
pressed the crowd, and the judges too! Showed he had
plenty of fight!"

"If he's friendly"—Rowdy grinned—"deliver me from my friends!"

Wells spat. "You've got a couple of mighty good friends, son. And neither of them are horses."

Luby was standing nearby. He turned, his elbows on the crossbar of the gate.

"You were lucky," he said. "Plain lucky."

Rowdy's eyes darkened. "Maybe. If so, I hope my luck holds all day. And tomorrow."

"It won't," Luby said flatly. "Your luck's played out! I've protested to the judges. I told them that allowin' a killer to ride would ruin the name of the show."

"Killer?" Rowdy wheeled. "Why, you—"

Bart Luby had been set for him, and too late Rowdy saw the punch coming. It was a smashing right that caught him on the side of the jaw. His feet flew up and he hit the dust flat on his back. Bart lunged for him. Rowdy rolled over and came up fast, butting Luby in the chest and staggering the bigger man. Bart set himself and rushed, smashing Horn back against the gate with a left and right, then following it up with a wicked hook to the head that made Rowdy's knees wobble.

Ducking a left, Horn tried to spring close, but Luby grabbed him and threw him into the dust. His face smeared with blood and dust, Rowdy came up, and through a fog of punch-drunkenness, he saw the big rancher coming in, on his face a sneer of triumph.

The man's reach was too long. Rowdy tried to go under a left and caught a smashing right uppercut on the mouth. Bart, his face livid with hatred, closed in, punching with both hands. Then Rowdy saw his chance. Luby drew his left back for a wide hook and Horn let go with a right. It beat the hook and caught Luby on the chin with the smash of a riveting hammer.

The big man staggered, his face a study in astonishment, and then Rowdy closed in, brushed away a left, and smashed both hands to the body, whipping them in with wicked sidearm punches, left and right to the wind. Luby threw a smashing right, but Rowdy was watching that left. It cocked again, and he pulled the trigger on his right.

Bart hit the dust on his shoulders. He rolled over, and Rowdy stood back, hands ready, waiting for him to get up. Blood dribbled from Rowdy's mouth and there was a red welt on his cheekbone, but he felt fine.

Luby was up with a lunge and caught Rowdy with two long swings, but Horn was inside of them, smashing a left to the body and a right to the head. Luby backed off, and suddenly, sensing victory, Rowdy Horn closed in. He chopped a left to the head, then a right, then another left. He smashed Luby with a straight left, and as Luby cocked a right, knocked him down.

Bart Luby lay there in the dust, thoroughly whipped. Reaching down, Rowdy jerked him to his feet and shoved him back against the corral bars. He cocked his right hand to smash the bigger man in the face, then hesitated.

Coolly, he stepped back.

"Nothing doing, Bart," he said calmly. "You started this, and you've had a beating comin' for a long time, but I'm givin' you no alibis. I want your eyes open because I'm goin' to beat your socks off out there in the arena. When I win, I'll win on the tanbark!"

Deliberately, he turned his back and walked toward the stables.

Bending over a bucket he bathed the dust and blood from his face and combed his hair. He scowled suddenly, remembering Neil Rice. What had become of the printer? In the hurry and confusion of being arrested, and then the rodeo, there had scarcely been time to think. Still, Rice might be back at the ranch by now.

What did Ben Wells have up his sleeve? Who were the friends he had mentioned, and had they effected his release to compete in the rodeo? He was puzzled and doubtful, and recalling the finding of the body in his cabin, he realized how desperate his situation truly was. Aside from Vaho, he had no evidence of any kind. To the sheriff, as well as to people generally, his story of killing a man in a remote canyon and then finding his body in his own cabin would seem too utterly fantastic.

Deliberately, he forced his thoughts away from that. First there were the contests. Each thing in its own time.

The next event was bareback bronc riding, then came steer wrestling and bull riding. After that, the finals in calf roping. Four men would compete in the finals: Cass Webster from Prescott and Tony Sandoval from Buffalo, Wyoming, besides Bart Luby and himself.

Bareback bronc riding was a specialty of Rowdy's, and he took a fighting first, riding Catamount, a wicked devil of a horse. Luby took second, with Webster a close third. Luby won the steer wrestling, beating Rowdy by two fifths of a second. Sandoval, the Wyoming rider, won the bull riding, and again Rowdy took a second, with Luby a third.

Sweating and weary, he walked slowly back to the corrals at the day's end. Tomorrow would decide it, but he was ahead of Luby so far. . . .

Morning came, and the air was electric with expectancy. Even the other contestants eyed Rowdy thoughtfully as he strolled quietly down to the stables. Silverside nickered softly as he came up, and Rowdy Horn stopped to talk to the horse as it nuzzled him under his arm with a delicate nose.

Cass Webster stopped nearby.

"This killin' stuff don't go with me, boy," he said quietly. "I don't savvy this fuss, but you stack up A-one where I stand." He ground his cigarette into the dust. "Luby washed himself out with me down to White Rock last year. He's dirty, Horn. You keep your eyes open."

"Thanks," said Rowdy.

His attention had turned from the cowboy and was

centered on Vaho Rainey, who was walking toward him, followed by the admiring glances of everyone.

"We've visitors," she said, "so be careful what you say."

His frown was puzzled. "I don't get it," he protested.

"You will. . . . Look!"

As she spoke, he turned his head. A small group of Indians was approaching. The first was old Cleetus, and the others were all men of his tribe, except one. That one, carefully concealed by a blanket, was Cochino!

"Glad to see you here," Rowdy told the Indians sincerely. "Very glad. If there's anything I can do, tell me."

They looked at Silverside and talked in low tones.

"They were here yesterday, too," Vaho whispered. "They watched you ride."

Suddenly, Cochino spoke to the girl, swiftly, with gestures. Her eyes brightened and she turned quickly.

"Oh, Rowdy! He says you can keep the horse! He is a present to you!"

"Good glory!" Beside himself with excitement and delight, he could scarcely find words. "But what'll I say? What can I give him?"

"Nothing. That is—well, he asks only one thing." Vaho was blushing furiously.

"What is it? Whatever it is, I'll do it!"

"I—can't tell you now. Later."

She quickly hurried away, and the old Indian chuckled. Cleetus smiled, showing broken teeth, but his eyes were grimly humorous.

An even bigger crowd swelled the arena to overflowing, and men crowded every available space. Pete Drago and his Demon Riders did their trick riding, their efforts augmented by the clowns, some of them rivaling Drago's amazing riders for sheer ability and thrills. The chuck wagon race followed, and an exhibition with bullwhips.

By the time the finals in the calf roping came

around, Rowdy Horn was up on Silverside and ready. This time he was following Bart Luby. The piggin' strings he kept in Silverside's stall were checked, and he brought them out ready for the tie. Momentarily, he draped them around the saddle horn, and at a call from Wells, walked over to him.

"Soon's this event is over," the sheriff said, "I want to see you."

Rowdy nodded grimly. "Sure," he said, "I'll look you up. It was mighty fine of you to give me this chance, Ben, and I'll be ready to go back to jail."

Despite that, his heart was heavy as he walked back to his horse and swung into the saddle. Thoughtfully, he stared out at the arena. Eleven seconds, the time he had made yesterday, was fast time. It was fast enough to win in many shows, but could he equal it today?

He picked up the piggin' strings and kept one in his right hand. The other he put in his teeth. Suddenly his consciousness, directed at the arena where Bart Luby had just charged out after his calf, was jerked back to himself. His lips felt something strange with the rawhide piggin' string. Jerking it from his teeth, he stared at it. Both strings had been carefully frayed with a file or some rough object. When drawn taut, to bind the calf's legs, they would snap like thread!

"Time!" Weaver's voice boomed out over the arena. "Bart Luby ties his calf in the record-breaking time for this show of ten and nine-tenths seconds!"

Cheers swept the arena, and Rowdy Horn felt something go sick inside of him. He heard his name called, and he twisted in the saddle.

"Cass!" he yelled. "Piggin' strings! Quick!"

Webster sprang as if stuck with a pin and thrust some piggin' strings in Rowdy's fingers. At the same instant, Rowdy tossed the frayed strings to the other contestant.

"Look!" he yelped.

He saw his calf leave the chute with a bound and take off down the arena like a bolt. Silverside saw it go and was in a dead run, heading down the arena. Rowdy's rope whirled and shot out, and he left the saddle with a leap, swept the calf from its feet and down deftly, swiftly. His heart pounding and the dust swirling in his nostrils, he made his tie and sprang free, arm uplifted!

Dead silence held the arena, and then, his voice wild with excitement, Weaver announced:

"Folks! Rowdy Horn, ridin' the great Silverside, wins the calf ropin' with the record time of ten and eight-tenths seconds!"

Cheers boomed across the arena, and Rowdy swung into the saddle and trotted his horse across to the judges' stand. His great horse reared high, and Rowdy's hat swung wide, acknowledging the cheers. Then, to the martial music of the band, Silverside dance-stepped across the arena to accompanying cheers. Then Rowdy turned the horse and rode him back to the chutes.

The memory of those frayed piggin' strings was in his mind. There was only one time it could have been done, hastily but deftly, and obviously planned for, and that had been while he was exchanging his few words with the sheriff.

Bart Luby had been sitting his horse, awaiting his signal, right beside Silverside!

Swift work, but it could have been done, for several minutes must have elapsed before Rowdy had returned to his horse. Only the sudden feel of the frayed place by his lips had saved him, for a snapped piggin' string would have meant too much loss of time.

He swung down and approached the tight little circle of men—Sheriff Ben Wells, Cass Webster, Tony Sandoval, Neil Rice, and others. And in the center of them, pale and defiant, his eyes hard with hatred, was Bart Luby.

Rowdy shoved through the crowd. "All right, blast you!" he flared. "Now you can have that beatin'!"

"Hold it, Horn!" Wells said sternly. "Step back now! This is in my hands!"

"All this talk is foolishness!" Luby declared harshly. "Why would I do a thing like that? I don't care what Webster says, I never touched those piggin' strings!"

"Same thing you done at White Rock!" Webster said flatly. "And you say I'm a liar, Bart Luby, and you've me to whip!"

Wells turned on him, scowling.

"Will you shut up!" he said testily. "That piggin' string deal was bad enough, but I'm arrestin' Luby for fraud, and for rustlin'."

"What?" Luby's face paled. "What are you talkin' about?"

"What I said," Ben Wells replied calmly. "This here hombre"—he gestured to Rice—"found Tom Slater's true will hid in a cabinet in the old Slash Bar ranch house. He also found a document there that had its seal removed. Meantime, I'd sent a couple of deputies with a posse back to hunt for that valley Rowdy told us about. They hit the jackpot and rounded up Jack Rollick and two of his boys. Rollick confessed that he helped you tote that body over to the Slash Bar, Luby, to dump it on Horn. Besides that, when I jugged Horn, I searched him, and found what he had plumb forgot— Rollick's tallybook showin' he rustled cows he'd sold through you and to you, even tellin' about the percentage he took off whenever you tipped him to good steals."

"It's all a pack of lies," Luby said, but his protest lacked emphasis.

"A search warrant got us into your house while you was down here," Wells went on remorselessly, "and we scared up that fake deed. Rice, here, he showed me how that seal was removed from one paper and used on the other. He also showed how the will you had was actually an old letter to you from Slater, but changed so to make it a will. You can tell by the creases where words were changed and added on."

Rowdy Horn looked up and saw Jenny Welman standing on the edge of the crowd, her lips parted. She stared at Luby, horrified, then at Rowdy. Abruptly, she turned and fled.

Horn had no wish to hear more. He was cleared now. Rice caught his eye.

"Boss," he said, "I did what I thought was right. You were gone, so I acted on my own."

"Fine," Rowdy said, "I'm glad you did." His eyes were straying, searching for the face he wanted. "You've got your job with me as long as you want it."

Vaho Rainey walked out from the stables, leading her palomino. Rowdy walked past Rice and stopped her. For an instant, their eyes held.

"Honey," he said then, "how many sheep would I have to swap Cleetus for you?"

She laughed. "He'd probably give you sheep to be rid of me. He loves me, I know, but now that I'm a young lady, I think I worry him."

"Maybe you wouldn't want to marry a cowman, even one with a ranch," he suggested.

"Why, Rowdy!" She laughed suddenly, her eyes dancing. "We've been engaged, or practically engaged, ever since we got Silverside!"

"What?" He stared at her. "What do you mean?"

She blushed, but her eyes were happy. "Why, I told Cochino that it was the custom of your people for the bride to bring a pony to her husband, and only the finest pony would do. That was what he was saying by the stables this morning. He said all he wanted in return for the horse, which he had actually given me to give you, anyway, was for you to take good care of your squaw!"

He chuckled. "Why, I reckon that's a good deal," he said whimsically. "The cheapest durned horse I ever got!"

# AUTHOR'S NOTE
# TOUGH MEN

Nobody will ever know how many people went west and just disappeared. Some were killed in Indian attacks; others died of thirst or were killed in stampedes or other accidents. The day-to-day work was rough and hard, and often a man was working alone. If hurt, he had to treat his injuries himself and survive if he could. Many a lonely grave beside the trail carries a marker from which the weather has long wiped out the name.

Relatives and friends in the east waited anxiously for letters that never came. Often, a woman thought herself deserted when it was only the west itself. That wild country had a way of absorbing people and leaving nothing to mark their passing. There were so many ways a man could die.

Sometimes, like Jim Drew in this story, they were simply too tough to kill.

In my novel *Conagher* somebody asks a stage driver if Conagher is a gunfighter, and his reply is, "No, but he's the kind the gunfighters leave alone, if they're smart."

There were many such men. They were not peace officers, they were not outlaws or gamblers, and they were not liable to be noticed by newspapers or historians. They were simply tough, game men who went about the business of existing. One such was Kirk Jordan, who ran gunfighter Billy Brooks out of Dodge; another was Colonel Frank North, of the Pawnee Battalion, known as perhaps the finest pistol shot of them all, but he never got into fights. I knew an old Indian in Arizona who was said to be past ninety (I never knew *his actual age, but his face looked old enough to have worn out two bodies) who could shoot the heads off Mexican quail. On several occasions when he needed quail for eating I have seen him kill two and three at a time.*

*He was not known as a gunfighter (although reputed to have killed several men) and would have disdained such a reputation.*

# Pardner from the Rio

Tandy Thayer rode up the river trail in the late afternoon, a tall young man with sand-colored hair, astride a gray horse. He drew rein before he reached the water hole, and looked carefully around as though searching for something missing from the terrain.

Tandy Thayer was slightly stooped as a man often becomes after long hours and years in the saddle, and his eyes had that steady, slow look of a man who knows his own mind and his own strength.

Turning in the saddle he studied the bare, burned red rock with a little frown gathering between his eyes. Here was where old man Drew's ranch should be, right on this spot. There was the water hole, and to the right, and not far distant, was the roar of the river. High upon the mountain to his left was that jagged streak of white rock pointing like an arrow to this place.

All the signs were right. The painstaking description had accounted for every foot of the trail until now. It had even accounted for every natural landmark here. Only there was no barn, no corral, no ranch house, and no Jim Drew. Nor was there any evidence that any of those things had existed upon this spot.

Tandy swung down from the saddle and trailed the bridle reins. The gray started purposefully but not too anxiously toward the water hole and sank his muzzle into the limpid pool. Thayer was thirsty himself, but his mind was occupied now with a puzzle. He shoved his hat back from his homely, weather-worn face with a quick, characteristic gesture and began to look around.

He heard the horse approaching before it arrived, so he faced about, turning himself squarely toward the trail up which he had just ridden. Another rider. From where?

The man was burly, a big man astride a powerful sorrel with a blazed face and three white stockings. His face was flat and swarthy, his eyes blue steel. He rode lopsided in the saddle with a careless cockiness that showed itself as well in the slant of his narrow-brimmed, flatcrowned hat.

"Howdy," he said, and inspected Tandy with a wary, casual interest. "Ridin' through?"

"I reckon. Huntin' an hombre name of Jim Drew. Know him?"

"Guess not. Was he comin' through here?"

"He lived here. Right on this spot if I figure right."

"Here?" The rider's voice was incredulous, but then he chuckled with a dry sound and his eyes glinted with what might have been malice. "Nobody ever lived here. You can see for yourself. Anyways, this here is Block T range, and they are mighty touchy folks. Me, I'd not ride it myself, only they know me." He dug into his shirt pocket for the makings. "How'd you happen to pick this spot?"

"Drew gave me directions, and mighty near drew me a map. He mentioned the river, the water hole, that streak on the mountain, and a few other things."

"Yeah?" The rider touched his tongue to the edge of the paper. "Must have slipped up somewheres along the trail. Nobody ever lived here in my time, and I've

been around here more'n ten years. Closest house is
the Block T, and that's six miles north of here. I live
back down the country, myself." He struck a match and
lighted his cigarette. "I'll be riding on. Gettin' hungry."

"You ride for the Block T?"

"No, I'm Kleinback. I own the K Bar. If you're
over thataway drop by and set a while. I'm headed to
see Bill Hofer, the hombre who ramrods the Block T."

Tandy Thayer was a stubborn man, and it had been
a long ride from Texas. Moreover, he had known Jim
Drew long enough to know that Drew would never give
wrong directions or invite him on a wild goose chase.

"That trail was plain as if he'd blazed it," he muttered. "I'll just have a look around."

He had his look around, for his pains, and over his
fire as dusk gathered, he considered the problem. His
eyes had already told him there was nothing to see. The
cabin, corrals, and stable so painstakingly described
were nowhere to be seen, nor was there any stock.

Hesitant as he was to pull out without finding
Drew, he felt that his best bet would be to try to land a
job as a rider for the Block T. He couldn't live on desert
grass.

Thayer organized the shadow of a meal from what
he carried in his saddlebags, then lighted a cigarette
and leaned back against a boulder to study things out.
Jim Drew was weatherbeaten and cantankerous, but he
was also sure moving and painstaking. Despite Kleinback's
statement, Tandy was sure Drew must be around
somewhere.

Picking up another piece of mesquite, he tossed it
on the fire. In the morning he would take a last look
around. If this was the place Drew had meant, there
would be some sign, surely.

Tandy had put out his hand for a stick and started
to toss it, when he caught the motion in midair. Along
the underside of that stick, his fingers had found a row

of notches. Holding the mesquite close to the fire, he studied it.

Two notches, and then a space followed by another notch. As he stared at those notches, with the cuts still unweathered, his mind skipped back to a camp alongside the Rio Grande below San Marcial where he once had sat across a campfire and watched Jim Drew cutting just such notches as he talked. It had been a habit of the old rancher's, just as some men whittle and others doodle with pen or pencil.

So, then. He was not wrong, and Jim Drew *had* been here. But if he had been here, where was he now? And where were the ranch buildings? Why had Kleinback not known about him? Or had he known?

Tandy got swiftly to his feet, recalling something he had observed as he had ridden up, but which had made no impression at the time. It was the position of three clumps of mesquite. He strode to the nearest one and, grasping a branch, gave it a jerk. It came loose so suddenly he all but fell.

Bending over, he felt with his hand for the place from which the roots had come. There was loose dirt, but when he brushed it aside, his fingers found the round outline of a posthole!

Grimly he got to his feet and replaced the mesquite, tamping the dirt around it. There was something wrong here, mighty wrong. He picked up a few loose sticks and walked slowly back to the fire.

He was feeding the sticks into the blaze when he heard another horse.

"Busy little place," he mentally commented, straightening up.

He stepped back from the fire, then heard a hoof strike stone, and saddle leather creak as of someone dismounting.

"Come on up to the fire," he said. "We're all friends here."

A spur jingled, feet crunched on gravel, and then he was looking across the fire into the eyes of a girl, a tall girl with a slim, willowy body.

She wore blue jeans and a man's battered hat. Her shirt, with a buckskin vest worn over it, was gray. She wore a gun, Tandy observed.

"By jiminy!" he exclaimed. "A woman! Sure never figured to see a woman in these hills, ma'am. Will you join me in some coffee?"

Her eyes showed no friendliness. "Who are you?" she demanded. "What do you want here?"

"Me?" Tandy shrugged. "Just a driftin' cowhand, ma'am. This water hole figgered to be a good camp for the night."

"Here?" Her voice was dry, skeptical. "When it is only six miles to the Block T?"

"Well, now. I'd started my camp before I knowed that, ma'am. Hombre name of Kleinback told me about the Block T."

Tandy was watching her when he said the name, Kleinback, and he saw her face stiffen a little.

"Oh?" she said. "So you've seen Roy? Are you working for him?"

"Huntin' work, ma'am. I'm a top hand. You know the Block T? Mebbe they could use me?"

"I'm Clarabel Jornal," she told him. "My uncle ramrods the Block T. He won't need you."

"Mebbe I'd better talk to him," Tandy said, smiling.

Her eyes blazed, and she took a step nearer the fire.

"Listen, rider!" she said sharply. "You'd best keep right on drifting! There's nothing in this country for anybody as nosy as you! Get going! If you don't, I'll send Pipal down to see you in the morning!"

"Who's he? The local watchdog? Sorry, ma'am, but I don't scare easy, so maybe you'd better send him. I ain't a right tough hombre, but I get along. As for being nosy, if you think I'm nosy you must be right sort of nosy yourself, comin' down here advising me to move on. I like it here, ma'am. In fact"—he paused to give emphasis to his words—"I may set up a ranch right here."

"Here?" Consternation struggled with anger in her voice. "Why here, of all places? Anyway, this is Block T range."

"Not filed on by Block T. Just claimed." Thayer grinned. "Ma'am, you might's well have some coffee."

"No!" she flared. "You be out of here by daylight or I'll send Pipal after you! He's killed four men!"

Tandy Thayer smiled, but his lips were thin and his eyes cold.

"Has he now? Suppose you just keep him at home in the mornin', ma'am. I'll come right up to the Block T, and if he's in a sweat to make it five, he can have his chance!"

When the girl swung into the saddle, her face angry, Thayer leaned back against the boulder once more. She was from the Block T, and the Block T claimed this range. Perhaps they had objected to Jim Drew's ranching here. And Pipal, whoever he was, might have done the objecting with lead. . . .

By daylight the setup looked no different than it had the previous night except that now Tandy Thayer studied the terrain with a new eye. Some changes, indicated by the mesquite bush planted in the posthole, had been made. With that in mind, he found the location of more postholes, found where the house had been and the barn.

Whoever had removed the traces of Drew and his ranch, had removed them with extraordinary care. Evidently they had expected someone to come looking and had believed they could fool whoever it would be. Only they had not known of the painstaking care with which old Jim gave directions, nor his habit of doodling with a knife.

Saddling up, Tandy Thayer headed up the trail between the river and the mountains for the Block T.

The place was nothing to look at: a long L-shaped adobe house shaded by giant cottonwoods, three pole corrals, a combination stable and blacksmith shop, the corner of the shop shielded from the sun by still another huge cottonwood, and a long bunkhouse.

Two horses were standing near the corral when Tandy rode into the ranch yard, and a short, square man with a dark face and a thin mustache came to the bunkhouse door and shaded his eyes to look at him.

At almost the same moment, a tall man in a faded checked shirt and vest came from the house. Thayer reined in before him.

"Howdy!" he said. "You Bill Hofer?"

"That's right." The man had keen, slightly worried blue eyes with a guarded look in their depths. He wore a six-gun tied too high to be of much use.

"Hunting a riding job," Tandy said. "Top hand, horse wrangler."

Hofer hesitated. "I can use you, all right," he said then. "We're shorthanded here. Throw your gear in the bunkhouse and get some grub."

The man with the thin mustache was nowhere in sight when Tandy shoved through the bunkhouse door and dropped his saddlebags on the first empty bunk he saw. He glanced around, and a frown gathered between his eyes. The bunkhouse had been built to accommodate at least twenty men, but only five bunks gave signs of occupancy.

As he was looking around, a red-headed hand came in, glancing at him.

"New, eh?" the redhead said. "Better throw your duffle back on your horse and ramble, pardner. This ain't a healthy place, noway."

Tandy turned, and his eyes swept the redhead. "That warning friendly, or not? Too many folks seem aimin' for me to move on."

Red shrugged. "Plumb friendly." He waved a hand

at the empty bunks. "That look good? You ain't no pilgrim. What about a spread that ordinarily uses twenty hands, and could use thirty, but only has four workin' hands and a cook? Does that look good?"

"What's the trouble?" asked Tandy.

"Maybe one thing, and maybe another. The trouble is, the boss hires 'em and Pipal fires 'em."

"Who's Pipal?"

A foot grated in the doorway and Red turned, his face turning a shade lighter under the freckles. The man with the thin mustache above cruel lips, and black eyes that bored into Thayer, stood there. He wore two guns, tied low, and was plainly a half-breed.

Warning signals sounded in Tandy's brain. Four men killed. Had one of them been Jim Drew? The thought stirred something deep within him, something primeval and ugly, something he had forgotten was there. He met the black eyes with his own steady, unblinking gaze.

"I am Pipal," the swarthy man said, his voice flat and level. "We do not need another hand. You will mount and ride."

Thayer smiled suddenly. This was trouble, and he wasn't backing away from it. He was no gunslinger, but he had put in more than a few years fighting Comanches and rustlers.

"The boss hired me," he said coldly. "The boss can fire me."

"I said—go!" Pipal cracked the word like a man cracks a bullwhip, and as he spoke, he stepped nearer, his hand dropping to his gun.

Tandy's left fist was at his belt where the thumb had been hooked a moment before. He drove it into the pit of Pipal's stomach with a snapping jolt, shooting it right from where it was. Pipal's wind left him with a grunt, and he doubled up in agony. Thayer promptly jerked his knee up into Pipal's face, knocking the man's head back. With Pipal's chin wide open and blood streaming from a smashed nose, Tandy set himself and swung left and right from his hip. Pipal went down in a heap.

Coolly, Tandy stepped over to him, jerked his guns from their holsters and shucked the shells into the palm of his hand. He dropped them into his pocket.

Pipal lay on the floor, blood dripping from his nose and his breath coming in wracking gasps.

"You better hightail," Red suggested. "He's a ringtailed terror with them guns."

Thayer grinned at Red and drew a smiling response. "I like it here," he said. "I'm stayin'!"

Pipal started to get up, and Thayer looked around at him.

"You get out!" he said harshly. "I don't know who you're runnin' errands for, but I mean to find out."

The half-breed glared at him, hatred a burning light in their black depths.

"I kill you!" he said.

Tandy seized the man by the collar and, jerking him erect, hit him two fast punches in the wind, then slapped him across the face. With a shove, he drove the gunman through the door, where he tripped and sprawled on his face.

"Look!" Tandy yelled.

He whipped a playing card from his pocket and spun it high into the air. In almost the same motion, he drew and fired. The card fluttered to the earth, and he calmly walked over to it and picked it up, thrusting it before Pipal's eyes and the startled eyes of Red and Hofer, who had come from the house. It was an ace of spades—with the ace shot neatly from the center!

Pipal gulped and slowly climbed to his feet. His nose still bled, and he backed away, wiping it with the back of his hand, an awed expression on his face. Calmly Tandy thrust the playing card into his shirt pocket and fed another shell into his six-gun.

"I don't like trouble," he remarked, "but I can handle it. . . ."

Three days passed quietly. There was plenty to do on the Block T, and Tandy Thayer had little time for looking around on his own, but he was learning things. The Block T was overrun with unbranded stock, and no effort was being made to brand any of it. Much of this stock was ranging far to the south around the Opal Mountains, where there was rich grass in the draws and plenty of water for that type of range.

Red Ringo was a mine of information. Red had been a rider for the Block T when he was sixteen, and had ridden for it four years. He then had drifted to Wyoming, Kansas, and Indian Territory, but finally headed back home. Three months before he had hired on at the Block T again, finding it vastly changed.

"Funny how a spread can go to pot in a short while," he commented to Tandy Thayer. "Even Bill Hofer's changed. He's thinner, cranky like he never used to be, and he packs a gun, something he never did in the old days. All the old hands are gone, and the last two was drove off by this Pipal. Why don't Hofer fire him?"

"Maybe he's afraid of him, too," Tandy suggested.

"Could be," Red agreed dubiously. "But he never used to be afraid of anything."

"When did all this trouble start?" asked Tandy.

"Well," Ringo said thoughtfully, "near as I know from what the old hands told me before they left, it started about the time the owner came out from Chicago. He came out and stayed on the ranch for a couple of weeks and then left, but whatever happened then, Hofer's never been the same since." Ringo leaned on the shovel with which he had been cleaning a water hole. "Another thing, Bill Hofer never had no use for Roy Kleinback before, but he sees a lot of him now. So does Miss Clarabel."

"What about Kleinback? He owns the K Bar, don't he?"

"Sure does. Rawhider, or was. Lately he's been doing better. Pretty slick with a gun, and a hand with his fists, too. He has three or four hands down there with him, but they don't amount to much aside from bein' crooked enough to do anything they are told if there's money in it."

Tandy Thayer hesitated and then with his eyes on Red Ringo, asked casually, "Ever hear of an old-timer around here named Jim Drew?"

"Drew? Can't say as I have. You mean an old man, or old in the country?"

"An old man. Cantankerous old cuss. Makes the best coffee in the world and the best biscuits. He was a friend of mine, a mighty good friend, and he's how come I'm here at all."

Briefly, Thayer explained about the letters that brought him here, and about finding the ranch site. Ringo listened with attention, and when Tandy stopped talking, he bit off a healthy chew.

"Listen," he said. "I come back here about three months ago. That was a month or maybe less after the big boss was here. I hired on, but the very day I started work, Hofer told me I was to work away from the river, and on no account to go near Moss Springs. He said there'd been some trouble over it and till it was straightened out, we'd stay away. Moss Springs is the water hole you mentioned. . . ."

Back at the ranch, Tandy sat under a huge cottonwood near the blacksmith shop and studied the situation through the smoke of a half-dozen cigarettes. No way could it make sense, so there must be something he didn't know.

Where was Jim Drew? What had caused the change in Bill Hofer and the Block T? Why was Pipal kept on? Did Hofer's new friendship for Kleinback have anything to do with all this?

In the three days Tandy had been on the ranch he had spent most of his time at work, and at no time had he seen Clarabel. Nor had he seen Kleinback. Pipal was around, but he remained strictly away from Tandy and never met his eyes if he could avoid it.

Obviously, the Drew ranch had been cleaned out because somebody did not want Tandy Thayer, the expected visitor, to find it. And they must have done away with Jim Drew at the same time. But why? What did they have to conceal?

Studied from every angle, the trouble seemed to have started with the leaving of the big boss, the owner—J. T. Martin. It was after that when Pipal came to the Block T, and after he came that the old hands started to drift away. It would almost appear that someone wanted the old hands driven off.

If there had been such an attempt, and if Drew had been killed or run off in connection with it, then there had to be profit somewhere for the instigators of the plot. What was profitable in this ranch? Cattle? And the range now covered with thousands of unbranded cattle, ready for the taking?

"So? It's you?"

At the sound of the girl's voice, Tandy glanced up and then got slowly to his feet.

"I reckon it is, ma'am. Like a bad penny, always turnin' up."

She stepped near him in the dappling shadows of moonlight through the leaves.

"Go away—please! You don't know what you're doing here! Tonight Kleinback is coming, and if he finds you, there will be trouble!"

"Sorry, ma'am," Tandy said easily. "I'm stayin' till I'm ordered off. I've got work to do. Mebbe Kleinback is the man I'd better talk to."

"No!" There was sheer panic in Clarabel Jornal's voice. "You mustn't! Please go! I don't know what hap-

pened to your friend. I have no idea! I think he just
pulled out and left!"

"You admit he was here, then?" Thayer shrugged.
"Ma'am, Jim Drew sent for me to come, so he never
pulled out. He wouldn't be driven, either! Ma'am, old
Jim was killed, and I aim to find out who did it!"

She was silent for a minute, her hand still on his
arm.

"Please!" she pleaded then. "You like me, I know
you do! I've seen it in your eyes tonight, and I saw it
the other day. If you'll go away, I'll go with you."

He shook his head. "That's a tempting offer, ma'am,
but I can't do it. I sure do like you. You're pretty much
of a woman, and a man could be proud of you, but I
wouldn't take you that way. I wouldn't take any woman
unless she loved me—and I reckon it would be pretty
hard to love a man like me. I ain't no hand with
womenfolks, and I sure ain't much for looks."

In the silence they heard the sound of a horse
cantering up to the house. Clarabel looked up at Tandy.

"It's Roy Kleinback!" she said, and there was stark
fear in her eyes.

Tandy caught her by the shoulders. "What's behind all this!" he demanded. "What's Kleinback to you?
Who is he?"

"He's nothing to me! I—"

"Hofer," Kleinback's harsh voice interrupted. "Who's
that hombre out there with Clarabel?"

The two men were walking toward the cottonwood. Clarabel stepped back, and her eyes looked like
dark, haunted pools in the whiteness of her face.
Kleinback walked up to her and Tandy, glancing from
one to the other.

"Hofer," he said as his eyes fastened on Thayer,
"you'd better fire this man. He's got some bad ideas.
Thinks there used to be an hombre name of Jim Drew
down at Moss Springs."

Thayer glimpsed a vague movement in the shadows and knew it was Pipal. He was boxed. If he started a fight now, he was finished.

"All right with me, if Hofer fires me," he drawled. "What about it, boss?"

"Maybe you'd better go," Hofer said. "Here's twenty dollars. That's more'n you got comin', but you've done a sight of work."

Kleinback was smiling. "Now, slope!" he said. "And once you start movin', keep goin'!"

Tandy Thayer offered no reply. He walked to the bunkhouse, threw his gear together, and saddled his horse. It was when he was saddling the horse that he brushed against Kleinback's mount near him, and against the coat that hung over the saddle horn. Something rustled in the pocket. On a hunch he turned and felt for the paper. It was an envelope. . . . No, there were three envelopes.

Shielding the match with his coat, he struck a light, and his heart gave a bound. All three were addressed to J. T. Martin at Nelson! Stuffing the letters back into the pocket he swung into the saddle and headed the gray toward the river.

The letters had been from Chicago, so in Chicago they believed Martin was here. And if Martin was neither here nor in Chicago, where was he?

Turning right near the river, Tandy Thayer headed south for Moss Springs. He did not ride fast, for he was in no hurry. The night stretched before him and he had only a few miles to go. In the meanwhile there was much to consider.

Martin had come to the Block T ranch and had probably received a report on the number of cattle there, but if he had known about all the unbranded cattle, obviously he would have been displeased. Suddenly, Tandy began to see more clearly, and the pieces of the plot began to fall into place.

Reaching Moss Springs he dismounted and made camp. Yet he was scarcely asleep before he heard the pounding of hoofs. Rolling out of his soogan he grabbed his Winchester and took shelter behind some rocks.

The racing horse came to a sliding stop, and he heard a girl gasping for breath.

"Tandy," she called softly. "Tandy Thayer! Where are you!"

"Here," he answered. "What's the trouble?"

She ran to him. "Oh, be careful! They've sent that man after you—Pipal!"

"They sent him? Who did?"

"Kleinback did. I heard him talking to Pipal. He told him to kill you, that you must never get to Nelson!"

"So?" Thayer went all quiet and still within, his mind examining the situation coolly. "Then he's guessed that I know what this is all about, or he is afraid I know." He looked around toward the dim outline of the girl's face. "Bel, what happened to Martin?"

Her breath caught. "I—I don't know."

"Bel, there's something plumb wrong going on here, and I think I know exactly what it is. Martin never went back to Chicago, Bel. Mail is still being addressed to him at Nelson, in care of the Block T. I found some letters to him in the pocket of Kleinback's coat. I think Martin was killed because of what he found at the ranch, or because somebody at the ranch was afraid of what he might do or know."

Clarabel was silent and he put his hand on her arm.

"Bel, did your uncle kill Martin?"

She jerked her arm away. "No!" she flared, and he could hear the anguish and tears in her voice. "No, he didn't! He couldn't have! He's always been good. Kind! He simply couldn't have!"

There was an answer here somewhere. All Tandy could see now was the vague, underlying plot, or what he believed was the plot. It would explain everything, and there was no other way that he could see for it to have been.

"Bel," he persisted, "what's Bill Hofer's tie-up with Kleinback?"

"I don't know." He could sense the honest doubt in her voice. "Uncle Bill used to dislike him very much, and I think he still does, but now Kleinback's around the ranch a lot and gives orders as much as my uncle does."

"Did it begin about the time that Martin left?"

She hesitated. "Yes, about then."

"Bel," Tandy suggested cautiously, "you think your uncle killed Martin, don't you?"

"I don't know, I tell you! But he couldn't have!"

"Bel, if your uncle killed Martin he's as guilty as any man, and deserves punishment if any man does. Now we've got to get at the truth of this, and I don't think your uncle did kill him."

Tandy hesitated, listening for sounds in the night. If Pipal was coming, there was little time.

"Was Kleinback at the ranch the night Martin left?" he asked after a moment.

"No. He was there in the afternoon. He and Uncle Bill had a fearful argument about something; then he left. I heard Martin and Uncle Bill talking for a long time after supper. Martin brought some liquor out, and they both had a few drinks."

That could be it. Had Hofer been drunk? He asked the question. "I—I don't know," Clarabel said, and Tandy could sense that this was what was responsible for the girl's worry. "I don't think he was. He rode down the trail with Martin to get him started right, and I don't know when he got back. He didn't get up until almost noon, I know, and he looked a sight. I think he slept in his clothes."

Tandy gripped her arm in a signal for silence, for he had heard a faint sound in the darkness, a faint dragging, as of a heavy body along the mountainside.

Drawing the girl back into the deep shadows of some mesquite, he listened. After a minute, both of them heard it again, a dragging sound, and what seemed like a grunt or a gasping breath.

Thayer stepped out into the moonlight, his brow furrowed. It was strange.

"So? We come together again, my friend!" Pipal's voice. "Make one move for your gun, and you die!" The renegade stepped forward into the moonlight. "Also the señorita will come from the darkness, or I shall have to shoot both of you!"

Clarabel, her face pale, stepped into sight and stood beside him. Pipal circled behind them and stripped them of their guns.

"Now," he said, moving away from them, "you will turn and walk toward the river. Bodies are so heavy to carry!"

"You're a fool, Pipal!" Thayer said.

His mouth felt dry, and he was weak in the knees. The half-breed was going to shoot, and any chance he took was a chance for the girl, too. If only she wasn't so close! Still, if he could get a hand on one of those guns, there might be a chance.

"Do you think Kleinback will let you go now, Pipal?" he taunted. "You'll be the only one who knows. You're doing his killing for him, and what will you get out of it?"

Pipal shrugged. "Plenty. Leave that to me, señor. I shall not forget Pipal. I never forget Pipal!"

In the silence, there was another sound, that faint dragging again. Pipal heard it also, and he started. He seemed to crouch a little, listening. His eyes dropped to the guns at Thayer's feet; then as the sound came again, he jerked his head around and Tandy's right hand dropped a little.

"Don't try it, son!" a voice roared out of the darkness. "I got him! Shoot me, will you? You drygulching—"

The voice was drowned in the roar of a heavy rifle as Pipal swung his gun toward the darkness.

Pipal jerked sharply, then took two steps forward and fell on his face.

"Jim!" Tandy Thayer could not believe it. "Is that you out there?"

"Who did you reckon it was? Sandy Claws?" The old man's voice was testy. "Come out here and fetch me in. I can't walk!"

In a few running steps, Tandy had reached the old man. His eyes sharpened as he picked him up and carried him back into the moonlight.

"Build a fire!" he told Clarabel. "He's been hurt!"

"Hurt, your Aunt Mariar!" The old man was exasperated. "I'm nigh starved, that's all! I was hurt, all right. Shot by that durned breed. He got me twice, once in the shoulder and the other time in the leg. I fell in the river, yonder, but caught me some brush and hauled myself out of the water. Takes more'n a couple of slugs to kill an old sidewinder like me! I crawled back up yonder in an old prospect hole with what grub I could get out of the house before they got back.

"Boy, they tore that ranch of our'n right down! Every pole and log of her. Then they dropped 'em in the river and cleared up the ground so's nobody but somebody like you would ever guess what happened. Me, I laid up there in that hole, trying to get my leg mended, me with nothin' but a mite of grub and my old Sharps. I caught me a rabbit or two and et them down to the hair, then tonight I heard your voice a-talking to this here girl. I been a-draggin' down that mountain ever since."

"Why did Pipal shoot you?" Tandy demanded.

"Why? Because I seen Kleinback and Hofer coming down the trail with that city feller. Hofer, he was riding with him, drunk as a hoot owl, but Kleinback was a ridin' back behind 'em a ways, following 'em, like."

Old Jim Drew told them quietly what had occurred, told them all he had seen, and Tandy nodded.

"I'd guessed most of it," he said, and swung into the saddle. "Jim, we're goin' to leave you here. We'll go back to the ranch and get a buckboard. Kleinback is still there, and I want to talk with him!"

The ranch was bathed in white moonlight when they rode up and swung down at the door. They halted at the sound of voices.

"Now is the time we'll sell, Hofer!" Kleinback was saying. "I'll start roundin' up tomorrow, and I'll get shut of them cows right away."

"I'll have no part of it!" Hofer said. "You got me into this, but I'll not get in any deeper."

"I got you into it?" Kleinback sneered. "Who killed young Martin? You did! What was your reason? Tryin' to rustle his cattle! There's a bad case against you, Hofer, but there's not a thing against me. I've got a clear trail behind me, and when I get the money for the cattle, I'll be free! I'll have plenty of money then, and not be tied to no two-by-four desert ranch!"

"You and Pipal," Hofer said, "between you, you ruined me. Between you two you ran my hands out of the country, and then after Martin was killed, you forced me to take Pipal on as a hand, so's he could spy on me and finish drivin' off the rest of 'em."

Roy Kleinback chuckled. "Sure. I've been running Block T stock back in the canyons of the Opals for the last couple of years. Holding 'em back there with no brands on 'em, so no evidence against me if somebody smartened up. Then when Martin came in and checked them draws and raised hob with you, I saw my only chance was to act fast. Then you up and killed him and saved my bacon."

"No he didn't, Kleinback!"

The two men sprang to their feet, Bill Hofer startled and staring, Kleinback with a sudden wariness in his eyes.

Keeping his eyes on Kleinback, Tandy Thayer went on coolly: "Hofer, you never killed Martin! You were drunk and didn't know any better, but old Jim Drew saw it! Kleinback killed Martin, then shoved the gun in your hand. He'd killed him with one of your guns that he lifted as he came alongside, and you too drunk to know better!"

Kleinback hooked his thumbs in his belt.

"That's a foolish notion!" he said. "You couldn't prove no such thing!"

"Jim Drew is alive, Kleinback," Tandy said. "He saw it all, as you know. Pipal shot him and dropped him in the river, but he caught some brush and got ashore. He's alive and able to testify to all he saw. You're through!"

Kleinback's elbow jerked back and his palm slapped the walnut gun stock, but even as the gun started to lift, Tandy Thayer shot him.

The big rancher sagged back, struggling to get his gun up while his eyes slowly glazed over and the gun fell from his fingers to the floor. Then Kleinback fell across it. For an instant there was utter stillness while the wheel on one of Kleinback's spurs did a slow turn.

"It wasn't me!" Hofer gasped. "Man, I—"

Clarabel was around the table and had him in her arms.

"It's all right, Uncle Bill! Everything is all right." She looked over at Tandy, and there was a smile for him in her eyes. "You were going to stay with old Jim?" she asked. "Why don't you? It would be nice to have you for a neighbor. . . ."

In the morning, Red Ringo grinned at Tandy. "He should have knowed better than to draw against an hombre slick with a gun as you," he said. "That was plumb suicide!"

"Luck," Thayer said honestly. "Pure luck!"

"Huh!" Ringo was disgusted. "After that card I saw you shoot a hole into?"

Thayer reached in his pocket and took out another card.

"Look!" he said. Spinning it into the air, he drew and fired. "Now take a look at it."

Ringo walked over and picked up the card. It was a trey, and all the pips were shot out. He stared at it.

"But you only shot once!" he protested.

"Sure." Tandy Thayer reached in his pocket and pulled out a deck of cards with all the pips shot out. "I shoot 'em out first, then always have one around. You ain't got any idea how many arguments they stop!"

# AUTHOR'S NOTE
# THE PASSING OF THE OLD WEST

The opening of the western lands went through many phases, and the settlement was very uneven. When some sections had become settled communities, other areas were just opening up, but wherever there was land, some settler would be sure to move in and establish himself. The old west passed reluctantly, changing with the times. Perhaps the end was in 1916, give or take a few years.

The last two holdups of stages by horse-riding bandits took place in 1916, one in Yellowstone Park, the other at Charlestown, Nevada. Charlestown—a wild, wild town during its brief day in the sun—was one of those towns born of misguided optimism. It is remembered, aside from the holdup, by the story of a sheriff who rode into Elko and stood at the bar having a drink. He shook his head in amazement several times and the bartender asked him what was the trouble.

He said, "Times are sure changing. This country ain't what it used to be. Why, I just rode all the way through Charlestown and nobody shot at me!"

There was a brief Indian outbreak on the Colorado-Utah border in 1915 when a small band of Paiutes led by Old Polk and his son Posey stirred up trouble in which at least one white man was killed and several Indians. The last known white man killed by Indians in

*Montezuma County, Colorado, was in 1886, but there was sporadic fighting all through the 1880s.*

*This area of southwestern Colorado and the bordering counties in Utah was one of the last to be settled in the United States. Here and there in other parts of the west, similar areas remained relatively wild and untamed after all the rest had been settled and life had to some extent been stabilized.*

# Bill Carey Rides West

The man on the flea-bitten mustang was a gone gosling. That was plain in the way he sat his horse, in the bloodstained bandage on his head and the dark stain on his left shoulder.

The horse was gone, too. The mustang was running raggedly, running the heart out of him to get the man away. The mount swept down through the pines and juniper, hit the bare slope, and stumbled, throwing the rider free.

He hit the ground hard, rolled over twice, and lay still.

Jane Conway had come to the door of her ranch house when she heard the rattle of flying hoofs. She stood there, shading her eyes up the hill against the sun. No rider was in sight.

"Anybody coming, Janie?" Her father's voice was weak, worn-out with pain and helplessness. "Thought I heard a horse runnin'?"

"I thought so, too," she agreed, puzzled, "but there's nobody in sight."

She went back to preparing supper. It would soon be dark, and they must save the little coal oil they had. There was no telling when they could get more.

Up on the hillside, consciousness returned slowly to the wounded man. Somehow, he had rolled over on his back, and he was looking up into a star-sprinkled sky. Cool wind stirred his hair, and he rolled over, getting his right hand under him. Then he pushed himself to his knees.

He felt for his guns. They were still there. Slowly and painfully, for his left arm was stiff and sore, he pushed shells into the two empty guns. Then he got to his feet.

The mustang was dead. He looked down at the little gray horse and found tears in his eyes, though he wasn't a crying man.

"You had nerve, boy," he said softly. "You wasn't much, and I hadn't had you long, but you had the heart of a champion!"

His rifle was in the boot, and he got it out. Then gently he worked the saddle loose. Shouldering it, he staggered painfully to a clump of juniper and dropped the saddle out of sight. For a minute he hesitated, staring down at the heavy saddlebags. He touched one with his toe and it jingled faintly. Gold. Well, it wouldn't do him much good.

Downhill he heard metal strike against metal, then the sound of a bucket being dipped into the water—the splat as the side of it struck the water, then the heavy gulp as the bucket filled. It was a still, cool night. Chambering a shell in his rifle, he started downhill.

No dog barked, and he was puzzled. A ranch in this lonely place would certainly have a dog. When he got closer he could see the house, small and neat, could see the rail corral, the log barn. But there was no bunkhouse. That simplified matters. Bill Carey wasn't wanting any shooting now.

He crossed the hard-packed earth, puzzled by the lack of light. It was early, judging by the stars, and he had been unconscious only a short time.

Something moved in the doorway, and he froze, his rifle covering the bit of white he could see.

"Stand still," he said, his voice low and hard. "I don't want to shoot, but I will if I have to."

"You don't have to shoot," a girl's voice replied. "Who are you? What do you want?"

A woman! Carey frowned, then he moved a step nearer. "Are you alone?" he said, low voiced. "Tell the truth!"

"I always tell the truth," she replied coolly. "Did Ryerson send you?"

"Ryerson?" He was puzzled, yet he lifted his head a little, some response coming to him as he heard the name. "Who's Ryerson?"

"If you don't know that," Jane Conway replied drily, "you're a stranger. Come in."

He walked forward, watching her keenly. The girl made no effort to move until he could almost touch her, then she saw the bandage on his head.

"Oh, you're hurt!" she exclaimed. "What happened? Did your horse throw you?"

"No." He looked at her, watching the effect of his words. "I was shot. By a posse," he added grimly. "I robbed a bank."

"Well"—Jane's voice was even—"every man to his own taste. You better let me have a look at your head."

He stepped into the darkness and waited, hearing her moving about. She went to a window, and he saw the grayness blanked out. Then another window. Then she closed the door. A moment later and a match flared.

They looked at each other then. Jane Conway was a tall girl with gray eyes and ash-blond hair. She was pretty, but too thin, a result of the heat and too much work.

She saw a big man with enormously broad and powerful shoulders, and the biceps revealed through the torn sleeve were a bulge of muscle. His face was haggard and hard, unshaven, with a brutal jaw on which was a stain of blood. This had evidently run down from under the bandage and dried in the stubble on his cheek.

He wore two guns, down-at-heel boots, and patched Levis. She saw the blood on his shirt and looked up at him again. Somehow she felt she had never seen so much raw power as she was seeing now. There was something, too, in the forward thrust of his jaw that made him seem indomitable. This man, she knew, would never accept defeat. He would drive on and on, against whatever obstacles there were.

"Sit down," she said sternly, "and don't worry. There is no law here."

"No law?" He seated himself, stared up at her. "What do you mean, no law?"

She smiled without bitterness. "These are the Shafter Hills," she said. "Haven't you heard?"

He had heard. The Shafter Hills. A patch of wooded and lonely hills, and among them the Hawk's Nest, the place where Hawk Shafter and his outlaws holed up. A nest of the most vicious criminals unhung.

Ryerson! The name struck him now like a blow. Tabat Ryerson! He was here! Bill Carey smiled grimly. He would be. Troubles never came singly.

"You mentioned Ryerson?" he asked. "What about him?"

Jane looked down at him. She could hear her father's even breathing. He was resting. That was something.

"If you were one of his crowd," she said, as though to herself, "you'd not come here."

As she took the bandage from his head and began to bathe it with warm water, she told him, "Tabat Ryerson is Hawk Shafter's right-hand man. He's a killer. Some say he's taking over from the old wolf. I thought he might have sent someone for me when I heard you coming. Then I knew if he had, you'd come on a horse. He said he was coming for me tonight or tomorrow—to take me to the Nest."

*     *     *

The warm water felt good, and her fingers were gentle.

"You want to go?" Bill Carey asked.

"No." Gently she began combing his tangled hair. "No woman would willingly go to Tabat Ryerson. He's a brute and a fiend. I'll kill him if I can. I'll kill myself if I can't get him."

He looked at her, shocked. Yet what he saw in her face told him she would do what she said. And she was right. Ryerson was a beast.

"He's been running this country," she went on, softly, "ever since the Hawk had his fall from a bronc. Shafter gave more and more power to Tabat. Every herd that's rustled means beef for him; every robbery means a percentage for him."

She began taking his shirt from his shoulders. There was no nonsense about her. She did what was to be done.

"He'll kill you if he finds you here," she said. "You'd better mount and ride when you've eaten."

"My horse is dead," he said simply. "Run to death."

"We've got several. There's a big black that will carry you. Take him and welcome."

"I can pay," he assured her grimly.

"I don't want stolen money," she replied. "Not any part of it. I'm giving him to you. A man as big as you," she added, "should do more than steal!"

Stung, he looked up quickly. "The bank foreclosed on my ranch. It was legal, but it wasn't right. He'd told me he'd give me more time. In the spring, maybe I could've made it."

"Listen!" Her voice quickened. "They are coming!" She looked at him anxiously.

"Go!" she said quickly. "Out the back! You can wait until we're gone, then take the black and go!"

He stood up, huge and formidable in the darkness as she doused the light.

"No," he said sullenly. "I don't run well on no empty stomach."

"Open up, Janie!" The voice outside was sharp and ugly. "Tabat sent us down to get you."

Bill Carey opened the door and stepped outside. He stood there in the vague light of the rising moon.

"Get out!" he snarled. "Get out—*fast!*"

"Who the devil are you?" a man's voice demanded.

Bill Carey's hand made a casual gesture, but the gun that suddenly filled it was not casual.

"You know the lingo this iron speaks," he said. "Get out! And tell Tabat Ryerson to leave this girl alone or I'll kill him!"

"You?" Anger crowded amusement in the man's voice. "Kill Ryerson?"

"Tell him to stay away," Carey continued, his voice ugly, "and tell Hawk Shafter an hombre from Laredo sent that word. If Tabat don't understand that, Shafter will! Now get!"

The two men backed their horses, turned them. A little way off they stopped, talking low voiced.

Carey watched them, his eyes narrow. "I got a rifle," he called drily. "If you two want to get planted, you can do it mighty easy!"

Their horses started moving, and he listened a long time. When he walked inside the girl had lighted the lamp again and was dishing up some food. He watched the steam rise from the coffee she poured into the thick white cup.

When she had put frijoles, potatoes, and cornbread on the tin plate he sat down and started to eat. He did not talk, but ate with the steady eating of a big man who was very, very hungry.

"Ryerson won't take that," Jane said warningly. "He'll come himself next time!"

"Uh-huh. I reckon he will." Bill leaned back in the chair and looked up at her quiet, rather pretty face. "But he won't come until morning. I know Ryerson."

He chuckled cynically. "Some men ain't so big as the shadow they throw."

Bill Carey got up from the chair and looked down at the rag rug on the floor.

"Better get some sleep," he advised. "I'll sleep here."

She started to protest, then turned away without speaking. In a few minutes she was back with a blanket. Using his holsters and rolled belt for a pillow, he pulled the blanket over him and stretched out on the floor. . . .

Dawn was gray in the eastern sky when he got up from the floor. After folding the blanket and buckling on his gun belts, he walked outside. Gray serpents of mist lay along the low places and wound back up into the trees along the mountain. The air was fresh, cool.

Bill Carey walked down to the barn and watered the stock. It was merely a matter of lifting a small board and letting water run into the trough in the corral. He forked hay over to the horses, and then studied the country with a knowing eye.

It was a good place for a ranch. There was plenty of water, and the gentle slope toward the creek was subirrigated by water from the mountain. There would be green grass here most of the year. A man could really make a place like this pay. It was even better than his own ranch, so recently lost.

His eyes were somber as he studied the dim trail that led toward the Hawk's Nest. So this was to be it. The old enmity between Tabat Ryerson and himself was to come to a head here, after all this time.

It was a feeling of long standing, this between him and Tabat. Five times they had fought with their fists, and four times Tabat, who was older and stronger, had whipped him. The fifth time, in Tombstone, he had given Ryerson a beating. Tabat had sworn to kill him if they met again.

Yet Tabat Ryerson knew, even as old Hawk Shafter

knew, that Bill Carey was a dangerous man with a six-gun. Had Carey been a vain man there could have been eleven notches on his guns.

Four were for members of a gang which had tried to rustle his cattle. He had cornered them, and in the subsequent fight all four had died in the mountain cabin where they had holed up. Carey, shot three times, had ridden back to town for help.

Three others he killed had been badmen who tried to run a town where he had been marshal. The other four had been gunmen, two of them Hawk Shafter's men, who had tried him out—one in Silver City, two in Sonora, and the last in Santa Fe.

When Bill walked back to the cabin the old man was awake. Jane was working over the fireplace, preparing breakfast.

"How's it, old-timer?" Carey asked, looking down at the grim, white-mustached old man. "Feelin' better?"

"A mite. My heart's bad. Ain't so pert as I used to be." He looked at Carey shrewdly. "You on the dodge? Janie told me some of it."

Carey nodded. "Don't worry. After a bit I'll be on my way."

Conway shook his head. "Ain't that, son. We'd mighty like to have you stay. Place needs a man around, and like I say, I ain't so pert no more." His face became grave. "Them outlaws is bad, son. Ride across my place every once in a while. Regular trail through here. Wasn't so bad when old Hawk was up and around. This Ryerson's poison mean."

Bill Carey was drinking coffee when he heard them coming. He was sitting there without a shirt, as Jane had taken his to wash. He got up, a big, brown, powerful man, and walked to the door. He was catlike on his feet, but when he got there, he put his rifle down alongside the door and leaned against the doorjamb, watching the horsemen.

Ryerson could be spotted at a distance. He sat a

horse the same as he always had. Carey watched him and the other outlaws with hard, cynical eyes. There was no fear in him, no excitement. This was not a new story, but one he could face without a tremor. He knew he could kill Tabat Ryerson without remorse. The man lived for cruelty and crime. He was nothing but a rattlesnake.

Three men. Carey smiled drily. Tabat must think well of himself. They reined in, and all three dropped to the ground. Bill did not move.

Then Ryerson took two steps, but froze and his face changed. Bill could not be sure whether it was a fear or fury that filled the man he faced as recognition came.

"You, is it?" Ryerson demanded. "What are you butting in here for?"

Carey straightened, and a slow smile came to his hard mouth.

"Maybe because I like these folks," he drawled. "Maybe because I don't like you."

"Don't ask for it, Carey," Ryerson snapped. "Get on your horse and take out, and we'll let you go."

Bill chuckled and ran his fingers through his thick hair.

"Don't wait for me to leave, Tabby," he said drily. "I like this place. Looks like the place a man could build to something."

"You and me can't live in the same country!" Ryerson snarled. "It ain't big enough for the two of us!"

"Uh-huh," Carey agreed. "You sure hit the nail on the head that time. And I'm staying. So if I was you, Tabat Ryerson, I'd fork that mangy bronc you're riding and take out—pronto!"

"You're telling me?" Ryerson's fury was a thing to behold. "Why, you—"

All three outlaws went for their guns. Carey's six-shooter bellowed from the doorway, but the thin, tiger-

like man on the right had flashed a fast gun, and his
shot burned past Carey's stomach. Tabat Ryerson's quick,
responsive jerk saved his life. Carey's second shot
knocked the tiger man reeling, and a third pinned him
to the ground.

Ryerson had leaped to one side, triggering his
pistol. He shot wildly, and splinters splattered in Bill's
face.

He whipped back inside the door, snapped a quick
shot at Tabat, then went through the house with a
lunge and slid through the back window just as the
other man came around the corner. Bill's feet hit the
ground at the instant they saw each other, and both
fired.

Bill shot low, and his bullet hit the big man above
the belt-buckle and knocked him to the ground. The
outlaw was game and rolled over, trying to get his feet
under him. The second shot was through his lungs and
the fellow went down, bloody froth mounting to his
lips.

Carey slid to the corner and, crouching, looked
around it. A shot split the edge of the log over his head;
then he heard a sudden rattle of horse's hoofs and
rounded the corner to see Tabat Ryerson racing into
the junipers.

He swore softly, knowing it had been only a begin-
ning. Tabat knew who he was now. He would come
back loaded for bear. Bill Carey walked toward the man
on the ground, his gun ready.

The thin, wiry fellow who had spoiled his first shot
was dead.

Carey walked back to the man behind the house.
He also was dead. Bill scowled. Two gone, but they
were two men who had been killed uselessly. Had it
been Ryerson, these two might have lived.

Janie was beside him suddenly, her eyes wide and
frightened.

"Are you all right?" she said anxiously.

Her wide gray eyes, frightened for him, stirred him strangely.

"Uh-huh," he said. "They didn't shoot too straight. Neither did I," he added bitterly. "I missed Tabat!"

"You think he'll come back?"

"Sure he'll come back—with help!"

She poured him fresh coffee and he studied the red crease across his stomach. Scarcely a drop of blood showed. The merest graze of the skin. But when she saw it, her face paled.

"You and the old man better get up in the pines," he said. "I'll hold it here."

"No." She shook her head with finality. "This is our home. Besides, Dad can't be moved."

"You're stubborn," he said. "A man could like a girl like you."

She smiled faintly. "Are you making love to me, Bill Carey?"

He flushed, then grinned. "Maybe. If I knew how, I reckon I would. I ain't so much, though. Just a would-be rancher who got gypped out of his ranch and robbed a bank."

"I think you're a good man at heart, Bill."

"Maybe." He shrugged. "I was raised right. Reckon I've come a long way since then."

He glanced at the hills. He was worried. Sheriff Buck Walters wasn't the man to give up. He had been close behind Bill yesterday. What had happened?

His eyes drifted down across the swell of the grassland toward the cottonwood-lined stream far below. The mist still lay in thin, emaciated streamers along the edge of the trees. A man could love this country. He narrowed his eyes, seeing white-faced cattle feeding over that broad, beautiful range. Yes, a man could do a lot here.

Regret stirred within him. That bank. Why did a man have to be such a hotheaded fool? He had been gypped, he knew. He had been tricked into asking for that loan, and he suspected there had been some rustling of his cattle. Well, that didn't matter now. No matter who had been in the right before, robbing the bank had put him in the wrong. He was over the line now, the thin line that divided so many men of the early west into the law-abiding and the lawless.

Reason told him he was one with Tabat Ryerson and the Shafter Hills gang now, but everything within him rebelled against it.

Thinking of old Hawk Shafter, he wondered. The old man was an outlaw, but he had also been a square shooter. Maybe, if—

Carey pushed away the thought. Getting into the Hawk's Nest would be almost impossible.

Sheriff Walters kept returning to his mind. The grim, hard-bitten old lawman would never leave a hot trail. Remembering the sheriff made Bill remember the gold and his saddle. Glancing down the empty trail, he turned and started up the mountain. His left arm was stiff, although he could use it. The bullet had gone through the muscle atop his shoulder. His head wound had been only a graze.

When he reached the junipers, he went into the thick tangle where he had hidden his saddle. The saddle was there, but the saddlebags were flat and empty!

Tabat Ryerson!

He had seen the outlaw come this way. Somehow, in hunting a hiding place from gunfire, the outlaw had found these bags, and had removed the gold.

Carey picked up the bags, and a white piece of paper dropped out. On it was written:

Thanks. You won't need this here where you're going.

Tabat.

Grimly Bill Carey swung his saddle to his right

shoulder and clumped down the mountain, staggering over the rocks. Might as well saddle that big black and be ready. When Walters came, he wouldn't have much time.

Walters! Ryerson! Carey grinned. If the two came at once, that would be something. He chuckled, and the thought kept stirring in his mind.

Walters could have lost his trail the other side of the mountain. Probably even now he was striking around for it. Carey recalled that he had ridden over a long rock ledge back there, and his trail might have been even better hidden than he believed.

If Buck Walters had seen him, he would have come right over here. And Tabat—

Carey dropped the saddle on the hard ground and, picking up his hair rope, shook out a loop. When he had roped the black and led the mount out of the corral, he turned to see Janie standing in the doorway watching him gravely. Their eyes met briefly; then she turned and walked back into the house, her face grave and serious.

He flushed suddenly. She thought he was leaving. She thought he was running away. Stubbornly he saddled the black, then swung into the saddle. The outlaw bunch might get here before he could find the sheriff. It was a chance he would have to take. His eyes strayed to the door again, and he turned the horse that way.

Janie stepped into the doorway.

"You got a rifle?" he demanded. His voice was harsh without his wanting it so.

She nodded, without speaking.

"Then hand me mine," he said. "If they come, be durned sure it's Ryerson's gang, then use that rifle. Be sure, because it might be a posse."

He held his rifle in his hand and, turning the black, rode off up the mountain down which he had come the night before. Three times he looked back. Each time the trail was empty of dust, and each time he could see the slim, erect figure of the girl in the doorway.

When he had been riding for no more than a half
hour, he saw the posse—a tight little knot of some
fifteen men, led by a tall, white-haired old man on a
sorrel horse. Buck Walters. Beside the white-haired
man was a thin, dried-out wisp of a half-breed. Antonio Deer! With that tracker on his trail, it was a wonder
they hadn't closed in already.

He looked downhill, then grinned and lifted his
rifle. He aimed and fired almost in the same instant,
shooting at a tree a dozen feet away from the sheriff.
The sorrel reared suddenly; then he saw the posse
scatter out, hesitate only an instant, and then, with a
whoop, start for him.

He was several hundred yards away and knew the
country now. He wheeled his horse and took off through
the brush at right angles to the trail, then cut back as
though to swing toward the direction from which they
had come. Whipping the black around a clump of juniper, he straightened out on the trail for home.

They would be cautious in the trees, he knew.
That would delay them a little, at least.

When he came out on the mountainside above the
Conway cabin, his heart gave a leap. Down the trail
was a cloud of dust, and the horsemen were already
within a quarter of a mile of the cabin!

Touching spurs to the black he started downhill at
breakneck speed, hoping against hope they wouldn't
see him. Yet he had gone no more than a hundred
yards when he heard a distant yell and saw several men
cut away from the main body and start for him.

A rifle spoke.

The lead horse stumbled and went down, and Bill
Carey saw a tiny puff of smoke lift from a cabin window.

The horsemen broke, scattering wide, but advanc-
ing on the house. The black was in a dead run now, and
Bill lifted his rifle and took a snapshot at the approaching horsemen who were coming on undaunted by the
girl's shot.

At that distance and from a running horse, he didn't expect a hit, nor did he make one, but the shot slowed the horsemen up, as he had hoped. Then he was nearing the cabin, and he saw two more horsemen break from the woods and start for him. They were close up, and he blasted a shot with the rifle held across his chest, and saw one man throw up his hands and plunge to the ground.

The other wheeled his horse, and Bill Carey fired three times as swiftly as he could chamber the shells. He saw the horse go down, throwing the man headlong into the mesquite.

Then the black was charging into the yard, and Bill Carey hit the ground running and made the cabin. The door slammed open as if it had been timed for his arrival, and he lunged inside.

Janie looked up at him, her eyes flashing; then as he crossed to the window, she dropped the bar in place.

A shot splattered glass and punched a hole in the bottom of the washbasin. Another thudded into the log sill below the window. Kneeling beside it, Carey put two quick shots into the brush beyond the corral, and drew back to reload.

Suddenly, from outside, there was a startled yell. Peering out through the window he could see a long stream of horsemen pouring out of the woods and coming down the hill.

Startled, Janie glanced at him.

"The posse!" he said grimly.

Her father was up on one elbow, cursing feebly at his helplessness. A man started from the brush, and Janie's rifle spoke. The fellow stumbled, then scrambled back into the mesquite.

Outside everything was a bedlam of roaring guns now. Somewhere a horse screamed in pain, and shots thudded into the cabin wall.

Jerking out his six-guns, Bill Carey sprang for the door. He threw it open and snapped a quick shot at a man peering around the corral. The fellow let go and dropped flat on his face, arms outspread.

The fight was moving away. Both outlaws and posse were mounted, and it was turning into a running fight.

Bill Carey crouched near the house, his face twisted in a scowl. Tabat Ryerson had come back to kill him. It wasn't like Tabat to run, not at this stage of the game. He would never leave now without killing Carey, or being killed.

Where was he?

Carey slid along the cabin wall, pressed close to the logs. The space between the house and corral was empty, except for a dead horse, lying with its back toward him. There was no movement in the corral. The dead man lay by the corner; another lay across the water trough.

The barn! Carey lunged from shelter and made the corral in a quick sprint. He went around the corral, still running, and dived for the side wall of the barn. When he reached it, he lifted himself slowly, trying to get a look into the window.

Carey could see nothing. Sunlight fell through the open door and across the shafts of an old buckboard. Wisps of hay hung down from the small loft overhead. There was nothing. No movement. No sign of anything human.

The firing had faded into the distance now, and was growing desultory. Somebody was winning and, knowing Buck Walters and the hard-bitten posse behind him, Bill Carey thought he knew who it was.

Bill Carey eased around the corner and glanced at the door of the barn. When he went through that door he was going to be outlined, stark and clear in the sunlight. But he was going through. Suddenly, he was mad clear through. He had never liked sneaking around. He liked to meet trouble face to face and blast it out, and the devil take the unfortunate or the slow of hand!

He lunged around the doorpost and went through

that path of sunlight with a lunge that carried him into
the shadow even as a gun bellowed. Dust fell from
overhead, but he had seen the flash of the gun. Tabat
Ryerson was behind the buckboard!

Carey stepped back into the open, firing as he
moved. He could see only a vague outline, but he
salted that outline down with lead and snapped a few
shots around it just for luck. He felt a slug hit him and
went to his knees. Then he was up, and standing there
swaying, he thumbed shells into a gun and heard
Ryerson's gun bellow. Something knocked him back
into the corner of the stall; then Tabat came out into
the open and Bill drilled him four times over the shirt
pocket with four fast-triggered shots, all of them within
the outline of the pocket itself.

Tabat folded and went down, and with his heart
shot to pieces, he still had life in him. He stared up at
Carey, his eyes blazing. "You always had my number,
curse you!" he gasped. "I hate the life of you, but
you're a mule-tough hombre!"

He sagged, and the light went out of his eyes. Bill
Carey automatically thumbed shells into his guns, staring down at the bullet-riddled body. The man was fairly
ballasted with lead.

"You're a right tough man, yourself!" he said softly.
"A right tough man!"

Carey walked out into the sunlight and saw Sheriff
Buck Walters and several of his men riding into the
yard. He holstered his guns, and stood there waiting,
his mouth tight.

Janie was standing in the doorway, standing as he
had seen her so many times, as he knew he could never
forget her.

Suddenly Bill Carey felt strange and lonely. Walters looked down.

"Looks like you had a bad time, Bill," he said
drily, "tackling all these bandits. I want to apologize,
too."

"For what?" Carey stared up at the hard riding sheriff.

"Why," Buck said innocently, "for thinking you was a thief! Old Hankins swore it was you robbed him, but he's so mean he can't see straight. When we found all that gold in Ryerson's saddlebags, we knew it was him was the thief. He being an outlaw, anyway, stands to reason we was wrong. Anyway, when we seen you this morning you was riding a big black, and that bandit didn't have no black horse."

"Funny, ain't it," Carey agreed, looking cynically at the old sheriff, "how a man can make mistakes?"

"Sure is," Walters agreed. "Even a salty hombre like you might make one." The sheriff patted his horse on the shoulder. "But there'd be no reason for him to make two!"

Bill Carey glanced at Janie Conway, her eyes shining with gladness.

"Why, Buck, I reckon you're right as rain!" Bill said. "I think if I was to leave this here ranch, I'd be making another one! Maybe you all better ride over here sometime and pay us a visit!"

"Us?" Walters looked at him, then at the girl. "Oh! Yeah, I see what you mean." Buck swung his horse around, then glanced down again. "Can she bake a cherry pie?"

"Can she?" Carey grinned. "Why, man, when we get married, she—"

He looked toward the door, and the girl had disappeared.

"Don't bother me, Sheriff," he said, grinning. "Can't you see I'm a family man?"

# About Louis L'Amour

*"I think of myself in the oral tradition—as a troubadour, a village tale-teller, the man in the shadows of the campfire. That's the way I'd like to be remembered—as a storyteller. A good storyteller."*

It is doubtful that any author could be as at home in the world re-created in his novels as Louis Dearborn L'Amour. Not only could he physically fill the boots of the rugged characters he wrote about, but he literally "walked the land my characters walk." His personal experiences as well as his lifelong devotion to historical research combined to give Mr. L'Amour the unique knowledge and understanding of people, events, and the challenge of the American frontier that became the hallmarks of his popularity.

Of French-Irish descent, Mr. L'Amour could trace his own family in North America back to the early 1600s and follow their steady progression westward, "always on the frontier." As a boy growing up in Jamestown, North Dakota, he absorbed all he could about his family's frontier heritage, including the story of his great-grandfather who was scalped by Sioux warriors.

Spurred by an eager curiosity and desire to broaden his horizons, Mr. L'Amour left home at the age of fifteen and enjoyed a wide variety of jobs including seaman, lumberjack, elephant handler, skinner of dead cattle, miner, and an officer in the transportation corps during World War II. During his "yondering" days he also circled the world on a freighter, sailed a dhow on the Red Sea, was shipwrecked in the West Indies and stranded in the Mojave Desert. He won fifty-one of fifty-nine fights as a professional boxer and worked as a journalist and lecturer. He was a voracious reader and collector of rare books. His personal library contained 17,000 volumes.

Mr. L'Amour "wanted to write almost from the time I could talk." After developing a widespread following for his many frontier and adventure stories written for fiction magazines, Mr. L'Amour published his first full-length novel, *Hondo,* in the United States in 1953. Every one of his more than 100 books is in print; there are nearly 260 million copies of his books in print worldwide, making him one of the best-selling authors in modern literary history. His books have been translated into twenty languages, and more than forty-five of his novels and stories have been made into feature films and television movies.

His hardcover bestsellers include *The Lonesome Gods, The Walking Drum* (his twelfth-century historical novel), *Jubal Sackett, Last of the Breed,* and *The Haunted Mesa.* His memoir, *Education of a Wandering Man,* was a leading bestseller in 1989. Audio dramatizations and adaptations of many L'Amour stories are available on cassette tapes from Bantam Audio publishing.

The recipient of many great honors and awards, in 1983 Mr. L'Amour became the first novelist ever to be awarded the Congressional Gold Medal by the United States Congress in honor of his life's work. In 1984 he was also awarded the Medal of Freedom by President Reagan.

Louis L'Amour died on June 10, 1988. His wife, Kathy, and their two children, Beau and Angelique, carry the L'Amour tradition forward with new books written by the author during his lifetime to be published by Bantam.

**A Preview of the Most Sought-After
Louis L'Amour Book Ever**

# SMOKE FROM
# THIS ALTAR

As a wonderful gift to L'Amour readers everywhere, Bantam Books has just published Louis's very first book, *Smoke from This Altar*, in a beautiful keepsake Bantam Hardcover edition.

*Smoke from This Altar* has never before been available nationally. As you read in Chapter 15 of *Education*, it was published more than fifty years ago for sale in Oklahoma bookstores. In the intervening years, *Smoke from This Altar* has become the hardest to find L'Amour title of all, with the few circulating copies from that small print run commanding top dollar from rare-book collectors. L'Amour fans have long been searching for it at their local bookstores, but to no avail.

*Smoke from This Altar* contains the best of Louis L'Amour's poems collected in book form. Like the short stories in the classic, million copy-selling *Yondering*, they are inspired by many of the events you just read about in *Education*—the author's experiences and memories of his wanderings around the world. Impassioned and heroic, the poems in this book are unique examples of Louis's storytelling ability as he writes about people and their love of the land.

For the Bantam edition of *Smoke from This Altar*, the L'Amour family has selected twenty additional poems by Louis that were not included in the original publication. And Louis's wife, Kathy, has written an introduction that we're pleased to preview for you here. In it she talks about the special place this book has held in the L'Amours' lives:

Louis's love of poetry and the English language was so strong and important in his life that it carried him through many dangerous and lonely days. At the time, poetry was the expression of Louis's most important thoughts and feelings. It was the first manner in which he wrote about his life, his views, and the places he had seen. Some of these poems got published in various newspapers and magazines, and though he made only a few dollars from these sales, they gave him the optimism to keep writing. . . .

Louis returned to the United States in the late nineteen thirties after years at sea, and moved in with his parents on a small farm near Choctaw, Oklahoma, that Parker, his brother, had bought for them a few years before. He was thirty years old, and knew that if he was ever going to make something of himself as a writer, he had better get started. He began writing short story after short story but they almost all were rejected. I think that he must have felt very tempted to leave again, to go back to the kind of life he had lived before he settled down and forced himself to think about his future. You can feel that wanderlust calling to him in several of these poems. . . .

During his travels he would occasionally compose poems, and it always seemed remarkable to me that he could both create and then rememeber them without writing them down; it seemed as if he could never forget a line or even a word. Louis explained that before the development of writing, poetry was one of the tricks ancient people used to remember stories. The rhyme and meter of each line would help you to remember the next. Because of this, poems that told a story, like those of Robert Service, were very popular with the hobos and sailors of his day. They were men with few possessions, some even illiterate, and so they were, in a way, like those prehistoric people who carried their literature in their heads.

When we first began dating, Louis gave me a copy of *Smoke from This Altar*, and through it I began to learn a little about the man who would become my husband and the father of our children. Many of the poems are about what he saw and thought and felt while he was in China and the South Pacific; and others are about places he visited that we went back to together. . . .

# LOUIS L'AMOUR

It's the best of the real West! Have you read them all?

| | | | | |
|---|---|---|---|---|
| The Iron Marshal | ___24844-8 $4.50 | The Quick and | | |
| The Key-Lock Man | ___28098-8 $4.50 | the Dead | ___28084-8 $4.50 |
| Kid Rodelo | ___24748-4 $4.50 | Radigan | ___28082-1 $4.50 |
| Kilkenny | ___24758-1 $4.50 | Reilly's Luck | ___25305-0 $4.50 |
| Killoe | ___25742-0 $4.50 | The Rider of | |
| Kilrone | ___24867-7 $4.50 | Lost Creek | ___25771-4 $4.50 |
| Kiowa Trail | ___24905-3 $4.50 | Rivers West | ___25436-7 $4.50 |
| Last of the Breed | ___28042-2 $5.50 | The Shadow Riders | ___23132-4 $4.50 |
| Last Stand at | | Shalako | ___24858-8 $4.50 |
| Papago Wells | ___25807-9 $4.50 | Showdown at | |
| The Lonesome | | Yellow Butte | ___27993-9 $4.50 |
| Gods | ___27578-6 $5.50 | Silver Canyon | ___24743-3 $4.50 |
| The Man Called | | Son of a | |
| Noon | ___24753-0 $4.50 | Wanted Man | ___24457-4 $4.50 |
| The Man from | | Taggart | ___25477-4 $4.50 |
| Skibbereen | ___24906-1 $4.50 | The Tall Stranger | ___28102-X $4.50 |
| The Man from the | | To Tame a Land | ___28031-7 $4.50 |
| Broken Hills | ___27679-4 $4.50 | Tucker | ___25022-1 $4.50 |
| Matagorda | ___28108-9 $4.50 | Under the Sweetwater | |
| Milo Talon | ___24763-8 $4.50 | Rim | ___24760-3 $4.50 |
| The Mountain | | Utah Blaine | ___24761-1 $4.50 |
| Valley War | ___25090-6 $4.50 | The Walking | |
| North to the Rails | ___28086-4 $4.50 | Drum | ___28040-6 $5.50 |
| Over on the | | Westward the Tide | ___24766-2 $4.50 |
| Dry Side | ___25321-2 $4.50 | Where the Long | |
| Passin' Through | ___25320-4 $4.50 | Grass Blows | ___28172-0 $4.50 |
| The Proving Trail | ___25304-2 $4.50 | | |

*In Canada add $1 per book*

- - - - - - - - - - - - - - - - - - - - - - - - - - - - - - - - - - -

**Ask for these books at your local bookstore or use this page to order.**

Please send me the books I have checked above. I am enclosing $____ (add $2.50 to cover postage and handling). Send check or money order, no cash or C.O.D.'s please.

Name _____

Address _____

City/State/Zip _____

Send order to: Bantam Books, Dept. LL 1, 2451 S. Wolf Rd., Des Plaines, IL 60018
Allow four to six weeks for delivery.
Prices and availability subject to change without notice.                LL 1 4/99